WHAT PE

GREN

In *Grendel's Mother: the Saga of the Wyrd-Wife*, an emotionally rich retelling of *Beowulf*, Susan Signe Morrison reveals the tragically human monsters obscured by the heroic bravado of the original poem. Only a scholar and poet steeped in Anglo-Saxon literature and culture could conceive of such a lyrical extension of the poem from the perspective of the women in the mead hall. Reading it opened the poem to me as never before. What a gift! *Grendel's Mother* is sure to become an integral part of every class on *Beowulf*.

Candace Robb, author of the Owen Archer Mystery Series and, as Emma Campion, *A Triple Knot*

This fascinating narrative is to readers today what John Gardner's *Grendel* was to readers of the 1970s. *Grendel's Mother* gives extra pleasure to lovers of medieval culture, since Morrison has enriched her novel with numerous treasure pieces taken from the earliest literatures of northern Europe. Poignant and yet exhilarating, Morrison's story surrounding the women of *Beowulf* has a universal appeal that will keep readers captivated from beginning to end.

Haruko Momma, Professor of English, New York University, author of *The Composition of Old English Poetry*

Finally, a creator in the long afterlife of *Beowulf* who puts Grendel's Mother at the centre of our consideration — just exactly where she belongs! And what a figure of knowledge, cultural intersection, power, and pain. Morrison's evocative text not only recreates and restructures the tales underlying *Beowulf*, but also weaves in a whole host of Germanic and Celtic material, including Norse tales and poems, medical recipes, charms, and riddles. She tells a realistic story of cultural and political intersections, with the focus on the woman at its core: a baptized Christian child, servant in a hall, a pagan queen, a wise woman, a bereft mother, an angel of death, a poet, a true leader and thinker.

M. J. Toswell, Professor in the Department of English at the University of Western Ontario

Grendel's mother of *Beowulf* is one of the most fascinating monsters in world literature, and she finds new life in Susan Morrison's fascinating narrative of love, strife, and sorrow in the age of the Scyldings. Drawing upon her own deep knowledge of ancient and medieval history, Morrison reconstructs a Norse world in vivid detail, creating scenes and characters for whom the great whale road, Valkyries, and earthy magic are terrifyingly real. Morrison's revisionary novel complicates traditional notions of heroism and villainy, evoking an eldritch, feminine power every bit the equal of the brazen warrior's might. Teratophiles, rejoice! With *Grendel's Mother*, Morrison has given us a "monstrous" woman worthy of our fear, our respect, and our love.

Robert T. Tally Jr., Texas State University, author of *Poe and the Subversion of American Literature: Satire, Fantasy, Critique*, CHOICE Outstanding Academic Title 2014

Since the era of Wagner, we have seen great public interest in Old English narratives like *Beowulf* and in Old Norse narratives like *The Saga of the Volsungs*. Unfortunately, popularized versions of these tales based on translations often perpetuate unfounded assumptions about what the past must have been like. More informative — and more enduringly popular — have been retellings by authors like Poul Anderson and J. R. R. Tolkien, literary artists who know the old tales in their original languages.

Morrison has a scholar's command of *Beowulf*. Like Anderson and Tolkien, she has hit on a method that brings ancient times to life more effectively than direct translation, which entangles the reader at once in doubts and difficulties. The most authentic recreations of early Northwest Europe weave material from many sources into an original plot. We may not understand everything that happens in *Beowulf*, but Morrison incorporates material from related songs and sagas to create a compelling story with the special appeal of a window on the past.

Geoffrey Russom, Professor Emeritus of English and Medieval Studies, Brown University

Grendel's Mother

The Saga of the Wyrd-Wife

Grendel's Mother

The Saga of the Wyrd-Wife

Susan Signe Morrison

TOP HAT BOOKS

Winchester, UK
Washington, USA

First published by Top Hat Books, 2015
Top Hat Books is an imprint of John Hunt Publishing Ltd., Laurel House, Station Approach,
Alresford, Hants, SO24 9JH, UK
office1@jhpbooks.net
www.johnhuntpublishing.com

For distributor details and how to order please visit the 'Ordering' section on our website.

Text copyright: Susan Signe Morrison 2014

ISBN: 978 1 78535 009 2
Library of Congress Control Number: 2015932685

A CIP catalogue record for this book is available from the British Library.

Design: Stuart Davies

Printed and bound by CPI Group (UK) Ltd, Croydon, CR0 4YY, UK

We operate a distinctive and ethical publishing philosophy in all
areas of our business, from our global network of authors to
production and worldwide distribution.

This book is dedicated to Geoffrey Russom, who first instilled in me a love for Old English and Old Norse.

Prologue

Once, in the long, long ago, the fisher folk and the fighting folk were one. They defended themselves from marauding wave riders. The grey time, before the fighting folk separated, held conflict and oppression, ill will, but also triumph and death.

The sea was the lifeblood for the fisher folk. They worked with the whale's path that birthed and killed them.

Some came to hate the seal-road. It drew them away from the softness of women. The fighting folk turned to tame the brine and control it. They built longships to teem the waves and conquer the salt flood and peoples living on those shores.

Who still carry those tales of that watery past? Only the poor fisher folk, who bide to the shore for survival, like lichens clinging to a rock. They sing the tales at sea, they croon the lays to their bairn, they chant the myths at the seaweed harvest. Clever hall scops, eager for gold, threaten to drown the sea songs.

Deeper, deeper, the salt lays are pushed beneath the waves, swelling on the surface, ripples that widen, smooth out and disappear, leaving no trace on the glassy face of the sea. The old stories that grannies and nursemaids tell in the night, whispered to soothe whimpering babes' cries, melt into the grey dusk like the people who tell them.

Listen, we have heard the fame of the mere-woman from days long since, how she fiercely combatted her enemies after she was first found helpless.

Long after the frost ogres fought with the gods, before Rome was sacked, when our ancestors, the northmen, pillaged in their longships and plied the whale's path, a woven basket floated on the salt-rimed sea. The basket, woven wave-rider, rocked with the flood, moon messenger. Foamy white peaks washed the suckling to the shore, sandy beach haven. Salt encrusted, the maiden slept, skin sun-tattered scarlet. Breathing in land wind, the girl-lady stirred, sensing the end of the flood, womb sheltered. That was an innocent child.

I. The Brine Baby

Me in those days my father and mother
gave up as dead.
Then a loyal kinswoman
wrapped me in clothes and kept and cherished me,
as kindly as she did for her children,
until, in her care,
I became mighty-hearted among those
who were no kin of mine.

Anglo-Saxon Riddle: *The Cuckoo*

The rime of night thaws in the pale day of winter gloom. My children cling to my skirts. I'm greedy for their sticky fingers, hot tears, and clinging hugs. I look out to the misty horizon, bide my husband's return.

Women often wait for men.

Here the wind hums the past, sings she-songs, which I gather as a child collects shells, treasuring them. I dream of my grandmother. She was no bloodkin. Yet her life flows in my veins, warms the foamy sea of memory. The hut where she first lived was cradled from the raw wind by dunes and bracken. One time, that bold woman chanted her story. She shared with my mother, her adopted daughter, deeds bold and grim. I listened to that sad song. One day I'll tell my daughter of that fierce lady. Those days will not fade, that glory will not be extinguished.

I stand on the shore where the frothy tide carried her many seasons ago. She had no past when she came from the sea. Her wyrd, her fate, had not yet been woven.

Chapter 1

The Seal Suckling

A. D. 377, the coast of Zealand, Scylding land

Seaweed hung drying from branches woven together into archways, like some crumbling monument of the giants on the sand. A woman placed the soggy leaves onto the delicate fingers of wood, from a basket piled with sea spears. The weed, once dried, would be used for fuel, emitting the pungent smell of the ocean within four snug walls, the home carrying the lingering scent of fish and brine. Some salty leaves lay on a compost heap to strengthen the weak soil and grow root vegetables. A few pieces would be eaten in a soup, hot watery salad, to warm bones in the chill midwinter.

As she set the weed over the branches, the woman caught the sound of a seagull's cry. Her home lay just off the sand on a little hillock of sea grass and shale. The gannet's glee was part of her song. As the mewing of the gull did not whisper away upon the wafting wind, the woman sought out the crying curlew. There she saw the soft seaweed, barnacled bed, of a marine monster. Leaving her work, approaching with caution, she listened for linnets along the lime lane. At first she thought it was a seal drifted ashore, something large, brown, and wet. She was momentarily frightened, then realized it didn't move.

She wiped her hands on her apron and walked toward what seemed to be a woven basket, a tiny covered boat, with only a small window on the topside exposed. Hurrying now, the woman pulled the boat further in from where it had been rocked by the waves. Through the opening above, she saw a mouth, teeth, little tongue, and heard a desolate whimper. In the sea cradle, washed up on the shore, lay an infant, cold and wet,

5

exhausted from crying and loneliness. Leather straps held down the boat basket's cover and she undid them, flipping over the top of the boat. The baby saw her and cried all the more, kicking now and desperately gulping for air. The woman touched its skin, briny and blue, frost bitten and forlorn, frozen and sore. She picked up the child, seal suckling, coldest of kits. The baby stank of sea and salt. The woman dragged the boat onto the shingle away from the tide and carried the mewling infant into the house.

The house was rectangular, twelve paces by eighteen. Heavy posts every few feet and parallel to the walls supported the thatched roof. The wicker-work sides had been coated in daub. At one end of the house were stalls for the animals — one cow, six sheep, two pigs, and three goats. A hearth lay in the center of the living quarters with an opening to the heavens for the smoke. The house smelled of animal warmth.

The baby fussed and the woman hushed it, talking quietly. The woman, Hildilid, had lost her first-born only months before to the wasting disease and had had no sign of a new arrival. Holding a child came easily to her, though not without a sudden stitch of pain, remembering the sweet dead infant who shriveled up despite her love. She lay the baby down, who was wiggling and kicking. Despite its arrival from the sea, the baby was only damp from the sea air and urine. The woman undressed it, the sharp smell of shit filling her nostrils. The poor thing had been left, it seemed, for hours, maybe days. Fetching some hot water from the kettle over the fire, Hildilid poured it into a big pan, along with some tepid water. She wiped the baby all over. It was a little girl, three half-years old, perhaps more.

The woman dressed the clean baby. Her own infant's clothes would not do, so she used the clothes promised for her own child had she grown older. Now the child was clean, dry, and dressed. The woman set on her next task, filling the girl's belly. Soup had been slowly heating on the hearth. Hildilid poured out a cup, tore off the heel of a fresh loaf of bread that she let soak in the brew to soften. The child gobbled the yeasty dough down — it disappeared immediately. She drank a glass of spring water in one gulp.

"Don't guzzle the soup, girleen," said the woman. "You'll burn your tongue."

Hildilid got a spoon, dipped it in the cup, and blew on the broth. The baby had soon finished the soup, and ate another piece of bread. It was warm in the room, heated by a fire, gold as Freya's tears. The roaring flames brought the child to life. She cried her first wail over the whale's sea on an alien shore, a second birth into a new life in a foreign haven. Hildilid picked up the child, too weary and confused to resist a stranger's succor, to nurse her. She sang a low, sweet song.

Dark eyelashes lay along the pink cheeks. The babe breathed deeply. Gently, Hildilid lay her down in the crib kept in the room. Her own child had been dead and cold only a few months; now a new one took her place. Hildilid stroked her hair, wiped away tears, and walked outside.

She drew the woven boat up by the house and took everything out of it. There were several leather skins that had once held a liquid, now dry. The poor thing had not drunk in a while. The blankets covering her were damp and salty. Only the one closest to her skin had been of a lighter, more delicate weave. In the foot of the boat, away from the little window on top, Hildilid found some objects. These she brought inside, along with the good blanket. These objects she put in her own marriage chest, under some well-spun cloths. The finely woven blanket she kept with her. Outside again she made a fire and threw the sea-soaked blankets on top. She watched them smoke. The boat she pulled behind the house aside the kitchen midden, piled high with oyster and mussel shells. She covered the boat with reeds.

Back in the house she went to check on the girl. She slept deeply still. Hildilid shifted the coverings around her. The child was warm enough now.

As twilight came, Sæwald and his partner returned home. Hildilid saw them pull up on the shore with a good catch. After Sæwald hung the sea supper to smoke above seaweed gleeds and bid his fishing friend farewell, he saw his wife emerge outdoors. He was relieved to see her, as she usually greeted him as soon as he returned home. He worried that she had done some mischief to herself out of grief for the lifeless child, even though it had been several months since that death.

Hildilid held her hands out to him. "Sæwald!"

"What is it, my woman? Have you come to ask me about our haul?" he asked, embracing her, glad to see her so lively.

"Come," she said excitedly, motioning him into the cottage.

"What have you within? A surprise?"

"Yes. For I have caught something at sea today as well." She laughed and motioned to the little bed.

Sæwald was stunned. For a moment he could say nothing. At last, "Whose is it?"

"She's ours."

He thought she'd gone mad. "Ours?" thinking she meant the dead baby. "How ours?"

"Oh, Sæwald, don't you see? Our child was taken away and we've been given this one."

"How did you find her?"

"She washed up here."

"Washed up? Like a seal?"

"No, no." Hildilid took him to the rear of their home. She held the reeds back to expose the boat.

Sæwald fingered it. "It's not of Scylding design."

"No, I knew that at once. You see, a foreign child. No one here will come looking for her."

"Someone else may."

Hildilid shook her head emphatically. "I've thought of that. Why would they then have abandoned her?"

Sæwald looked at the boat again. He touched it, examining the weave. "It could be Frankish, or of Heathobard design."

"What does it matter? No one knows she's here."

"The king will have to know."

"The king!" Hildilid was exasperated. "How could he deny us her?"

"I don't know," said Sæwald slowly. Now they were back in the cottage. The child sighed in her sleep. Her eyelids flickered and she awoke. Seeing the two faces gazing at her in the awe and hope of love, she began to cry. Hildilid held and rocked her. Sæwald went to one end of the room and came back with a little rattle shaped from wood into a seal. He had whittled it for his own bairn, destined for death.

The child cried, yet looked with interest. Then she grabbed it. She gazed at Sæwald, seeming to acknowledge him with her eyes, deep pools of pleading.

"I'll speak to the king myself, if need be," he assured his wife after a moment.

Chapter 2

A Kingly Command

A few weeks later Hildilid's brother, one of the royal coast guard, visited. "Sister?" he cried as he stepped onto their beach. "Sister!"

She emerged from the house. Behind her appeared a small child, still almost a baby, though walking competently.

Scyldtheow was amazed. Had his niece come back to life?

"Hello, brother. What news do you bring us?" asked Hildilid.

At last he managed to say, "What news have you for me, sister?"

The girl held her mother's hand and pressed herself into her skirts.

"We have our daughter again."

"She died."

"The sea coughed up another. The gods have returned her."

"Do not speak in riddles."

"She washed up on our shore." Hildilid showed the boat. The girl was now sitting in the sand, digging with a shell.

"Does she speak?"

"She babbles in her native tongue."

"Which is —?"

"I don't know. Neither does Sæwald," she said, pointing to her man who had just arrived.

"Good even, brother."

"And to you. I see the sea gave birth."

"And we are the midwives."

"I've seen the boat, brother," said Scyldtheow cautiously.

"And?"

"It is a foreign vessel."

"I know that. The child was rejected. She came here alone and in need. We want her for our own."

Scyldtheow was no sister-hater, kin-killer. He was a king-counselor, hero-helper. Pausing, he chose his words carefully. "I shall have to tell the king."

Hildilid cried out so that the child looked up briefly from her game. "No! Why must he know? What can it matter to him?"

Scyldtheow spoke in his official capacity. "All aliens must be made known to the king." Then, in a softer tone, "I'm sure it will turn out favorably." Though he was not certain of that.

When next Scyldtheow went to the king's home, a large and simple hall, he took an opportunity to speak to him. Back at the beer byre, the sea-scout told what he had found.

"I have news of an alien invasion, your majesty," he said.

"Indeed?" said Hrothgar, son of Healfdene. "Yet your demeanor is calm and relaxed. Are they friends?"

"I think so, my Lord."

"Who is it, Scyldtheow?" asked the queen mother, Ealhhild, Healfdene's widow. Healfdene had been king. Now his son, Hrothgar, reigned. He was near forty half-years old. So time was measured, by half-year or season, two each lunar year.

"A child."

"A child?" asked Hrothgar.

"To be more precise, a baby. Well, older than a tiny baby. Perhaps three half-years in age."

The queen mother smiled. "Where is this frightening creature?"

"At my sister's, Hildilid, my lady."

"Ah." Hildilid had grown up at court, such as it was. Hrothgar's kingdom was of several thousand persons, not including the communities he'd conquered overseas or distant since he took the throne a few years earlier. While some Scyldings were court members and others fished and farmed, there was a fluidity about the society. A farmer, if a likely warrior, could easily become beloved at court. Even those at court had to keep their families alive through farming or fishing.

Still, Hildilid would normally have married a retainer or his son, as her own father had been a court counselor.

Instead, she'd fallen in love with Sæwald. Hildilid was one of several daughters, and not the favorite, so her father let her marry her beloved. Though familiar with court ways, she was happy to be exiled from them. They were lucky lovers. Poets play and scops sing of woeful wedlock, keening couples. Theirs was a contented coupling.

"How did Hildilid acquire the child?" Hrothgar asked.

"She floated on to shore some three weeks ago." All the retainers listened. "She was in a woven cradle-boat, with leather skins of milk and some food. My sister, as you know, lost her baby recently. She wants to keep this child for her own."

Hrothgar said, "I see no problem with that."

Ealhhild interjected, "Who lost the child? A Scylding?"

Scyldtheow hesitated. "No, lady. She seems to be of foreign birth."

"That could be a problem."

"How, Mother? Surely, even if of foreign birth, the baby has been abandoned, they don't want her now."

"It could be a trap," said the queen.

"Nonsense!"

"Is it, my son? What if the Heathobards, subdued only a few years ago, want to pick a quarrel with you, setting this girl among us to use at a later date? They could say we stole her. What if she is the king's child?"

"Mother, these are fantasies you spin."

"I have seen enough bloodshed in my time to know that one innocent action, committed from generous desires, could seed later destruction."

Hrothgar thought and then pronounced, "Let us go then to your sister's home. We will see the child for ourselves."

The following day, the queen mother, Hrothgar, his retainer Unferth, Unferth's brother Coifi the shaman, and Scyldtheow set out for the beach on horseback. They were the legal leaders, powerful persons. Once another king, Solomon, had decided a baby's brethren, foundling's family.

"What would you suggest, Mother, if she is a spy?" asked Hrothgar playfully. "Send her back to the fishes?"

"Don't be ridiculous, my son. I am not a cruel fiend. We would have to take counsel then, of course."

Hildilid and Sæwald were at home awaiting the royal visit. No introductions were necessary.

"Hildilid," said the queen, "I hear you've had good fortune."

"Yes, lady. My daughter has arrived. A new one to heal the pain of the lost babe."

"May we see her?"

Hildilid returned from the cot carrying the girl, who looked worriedly at all the serious faces. She said, "Mama!" and held on to Hildilid tightly.

"Does she speak at all?"

"When she came, lady, she babbled in her native tongue. We don't know what it was. Now she's starting to speak our words. Slowly, but clearly."

"A wise child," said the queen.

Hrothgar decided to take charge. "Let us see the boat she came in." Sæwald pulled the vessel from the bracken. All examined it. "What is your conclusion?" Hrothgar asked of Scyldtheow.

"Sæwald and I agree that it is of a foreign hand. Frankish, perhaps, possibly Heathobard."

Ealhhild look triumphantly towards her son. Hrothgar hurried on, "And was she fit when she arrived?"

"She was tired and cold, hungry and dirty," said Hildilid.

"How long had she been alone?"

"I can't judge. From her swaddling clothes, I'd say at least a day, perhaps two or three."

"That means nothing," Scyldtheow interjected. "She could

have been dropped from a ship at sea, any sea, from anywhere. No one could possibly know she'd land here."

"True," agreed the queen reluctantly. "Were there any hints as to her parentage in the boat?"

"Only these leather bags which had had milk in them. And the blankets covering her."

The queen's eyes lighted up. "Blankets! Let us see!"

Hildilid went in to fetch the one surviving blanket the girl slept with every night. When Ealhhild took it, the child whimpered. "Hush, hush," whispered Hildilid.

"It is finely woven. It could come from anywhere," the queen said at last. "Even from here." She looked at Hildilid. "Was she covered in one blanket only?"

"I burned the others," Hildilid said. "They were so covered in spray and salt."

The queen looked at Hildilid deeply. "Was there nothing else?"

Hildilid gazed back at her steadily. "Only her shit-covered cloths. And those I burned too."

"Mother," said Hrothgar, "I think we can see what happened. A loving parent had to abandon her, for some reason. Disease, perhaps? Yet the child has clearly brought none here. Or famine? Yet she had food enough. The fear of attack? Who knows? The parents wanted her to be loved and helped. I see no problem in her becoming Hildilid and Sæwald's child. Many children are adopted by foster parents. It causes no anxiety."

"Not alien children of unknown origins — in times like these!" said his mother anxiously.

"Would you have us send her back to the sea?" asked Hildilid in tears.

The queen looked at Hildilid a long time. "No. I would not have that. I simply want to say that an alien will ultimately bring about trouble, intentionally or no. Remember Gudrun, carrying stones, desiring death, floated on the swan's back to King Jonakr.

Later it brought about her daughter's death, trampled by horses, and the stoning of her sons. That was no happy voyage."

"Gudrun lives in the scop's song, Mother, not in reality. Besides, she's a child, Mother. And a sweet one at that," said Hrothgar, as the child had shyly smiled at him. "She can do us no harm." Then, turning to the parents, "What will you call her?"

"We were thinking Brimhild," said Sæwald, "for battle of the sea."

"Let us go then," said Ealhhild. "But watch the horizon, Scyldtheow. Sails of foreigners may come to rescue her. Then, though sold into slavery, I will be right."

"My mother is a little overcautious, Hildilid and Sæwald. Do not mind her. Bring the child to the court when she is older. Perhaps we can make a good marriage for her."

Hildilid beamed and Sæwald bowed in thanks. That was a good king!

How the babe had survived, no Scylding could understand. Some thought she had been left near shore by a Dane, wanton woman, willing her people to take the bairn for an abandoned foreigner. Yet the cradle was created by an alien hand. How did she live? What did she eat while on Mother Sea, home of our engendering, until the icy brine calls us home to that grave? Her milky foam, the wave's teat? The mere was her mother — coddling her cuttlefish, a little girl with no kin or kind. Was she forgotten? Floating by accident? Stolen by sea monsters? Left by her parents, who shed salt tears into the brine at the tide's tugging? Abandoned for her own safety, like Moses in the bullrushes, a girl child to deliver her people? Fluctuating flood drifted the briny babe, the mere-maid, to the shifting sands of Scyldying shores.

After the royal party had departed, Hildilid and Sæwald embraced in relief. Sæwald stayed on the beach with the child, looking for crabs. Hildilid returned into the house. Listening to their voices outside, she went to her wedding chest. All their court clothes and fine jewelry were packed away as a dowry, never touched. Beneath one fine gown were Brimhild's treasures, the objects from the foot of the plaited boat. Hildilid picked them up. A silver spoon, long-handled, with strange marks repeated on it, a vertical line with a horizontal one cutting through it at right angles. Each line was of the same length. Writing was engraved around the bowl of the spoon. A book in leather with several illuminations — one of a mother and baby. Perhaps it was a portrait of Brimhild's mother. And pieces of gold jewelry. All these wrapped up in a fine woven shawl. Hildilid placed them carefully back into the chest. One day she would give them to Brimhild, when she was ready to hear of her origins. For each one must know where she comes from, to see where she is headed.

Chapter 3

Gobban's God

Hildilid's great-aunt, Ælfsciene, would come to visit. I have heard tell she could utter charms which worked wonders. She saved children from defeating disease, women from lingering labor, men from wicked wounds. She was said to have the ability to see the future. When she first met Brimhild, only a few months after the child washed up, Aunt Ælfsciene put her hand on Brimhild's forehead and muttered some words. She seemed to go into a trance. Hildilid watched and was frightened.

"Aunt Ælfsciene," she cried, as the trance subsided, "what do you see?"

"She came from water, and will return to water." At that, Aunt Ælfsciene seemed to awaken and beamed a smile. "Aren't you a sweet girl?" she crooned, and Brimhild smiled back at her.

Half-year followed half-year, season upon season. Brimhild soon mastered the language spoken by her parents. Growing up on the beach was a paradise for the child. She learned to dig for clams, to net fish in the shallow waters, even to swim in the brief summer time, a skill most men did not possess. Although her babyhood sang like a magic rhyme, suggestive, elusive, unknown, her childhood was not the stuff of scops, who sang to royal visitors in gold-laden halls, nor murmured on the foamy seas by sailors mending ropes, nor even hummed by flaxen-haired mothers or wily crones, lulling their bairns to sleep. Her life was no heroic adventure of daring and greatness, only the humble journey from cottage to garden, from shallow waters to the kitchen's cracking fire and iron pot, from kelp plot to the dune above their home, to gaze towards the horizon, to wonder about the beyond. So it is with those lost at sea only to be saved through some twist of interlaced fate. Those saved either shun the brine for the terror drowns them still, or cling to the icy wave, intent on conquering the frozen grip of the white flecked sea. So it was with Brimhild, wandering ever and again to the shoreline, unable to leave it, captured by its power.

Her mother asked her what she remembered of her babyhood.

"The earliest I remember, Mother, is your face. And the sea...."

"You do remember that? The sea?"

"Yes, Mother. The salt and waves and wind. I was rocked in the sea."

That vessel voyage was a second birth. Her first genesis had been in salt water too.

"I have heard tell," began Hildilid, "of a baby found on the waters, whispering rushes accompanied his cries. The king's daughter saved him from the stream's sorrows by embracing his birth basket. That boy grew to save his people, the hated Hebrews, suffering slaves. He was God's man, Thor's thane, Odin's worshipper. He returned to the sea, parted waters.

"A maiden, too, came from the sea. Glistening and gleaming, she glowed from her sea-birth, fully formed, lovely lady. She came to lead lovers, players with passion.

"All these came from the sea, like you, Brimhild. One day you may lead your people, rule waves. Ælfsciene believes you'll return to water. Perhaps you'll take a trip over sea spray, conquer killers, promote peace."

"Mother!" chided Brimhild. "You act like I'm a princess."

"You are to me."

"I am a fisherman's daughter, kin of my mother, Hildilid's hearth child."

"Yes, you are my child, Hildilid's heart. Yet you spring from alien loins, a faraway womb."

One day Sæwald returned from a fishing voyage of a few weeks' duration. With him was a strange fish — a monk. Hildilid asked who he was.

"I'm not sure. His name is Gobban. He's an Irish priest. He

speaks the Danish tongue in a basic way. From what I understood, he is wandering to find God."

"God? Does he mean Thor? Or Odin?"

"I know not. Yet he was lost at sea in his tiny boat, one he'd made himself. If we had not happened upon him, he would have died of exposure within a day. He had no food or fresh water and was exhausted. At first he refused to climb into our boat. The seas were high. We threw a rope and hauled him in. Since then he claims he wanted God to save him. I know not his god. I said perhaps we were sent by that god to rescue him. I think he wanted to suffer more."

"A strange creature."

"Indeed. He is gentle and does no harm. I think he should stay with us until he is able to travel."

Hildilid agreed. She set up a place for him to sleep in the animal shed. The straw was thick and clean. It would keep him warm.

Gobban was grateful for all the kindness they showed him. At first, Brimhild was frightened by him. His fair hair was fashioned strangely, shaved in front with flowing locks behind. He wore robes of rough dark cloth. Gobban made all sorts of outlandish gestures before each meal, speaking in a tongue neither Hildilid nor Sæwald recognized.

Gobban had been raised with many brothers and sisters and knew how to make funny faces to little ones. His simple speech was easily followed by the girl who taught him new words, as children will.

One night, after they had eaten, he told them of his God in fractured speech. "He is not bad God. He good God. He one God."

Sæwald asked, puzzled, "You mean only *he* exists as God? There aren't *many* gods? We have the god of thunder, the god of fire, the goddess of fertility."

"We have one God only. He is three Gods."

"So you do have more than one!"

"No, no. He is one God. He has three....?"

"Three hands?"

"Yes. No. Too difficult."

"Please explain," said Brimhild, who had only recently begun to comprehend the religious system of the Scyldings. "Here we praise Odin for his bravery and knowledge."

"My God know all. My God father. My God son."

"Whose son?"

"God is father and son."

"Impossible!" exclaimed Sæwald. "That would be incest!"

"That's certainly not unheard of among our gods, Sæwald," Hildilid pointed out, smiling. She turned to the monk. "Gobban," she asked gently, "how can the father God and son God be different and the same?"

"They are same. One."

"I don't understand," said Sæwald.

"I see, Daddy," said Brimhild. "Maybe his God turns into the father or the son whenever it suits him. If he needs to talk to a king, he'd be the father, if he needs to talk to a child, he's the son."

Gobban smiled. Though Brimhild had not gotten it right, she understood that something happened beyond the normal process of life. "Girl understand best."

Brimhild smiled proudly.

Then Hildilid asked, "Who is the third God? Number three? Who?"

Gobban thought for a moment. "Difficult to say." He hit his chest. "Inside. Within."

The three worshippers of Odin were lost. "But," said Brimhild, "who is the mother of God? You said there is a father and a son."

"Yes, yes. Little baby Jesus had mother Mary."

"Who is Jesus?" asked Brimhild.

"Son God. He born by woman. Good woman. Clean woman."

"Clean woman?" asked Sæwald.

"No man," explained Gobban.

"You mean she was unmarried?" asked Hildilid. Illegitimate births were hardly unknown in her culture.

"No, no. Special woman. Clean. No man."

"You mean a virgin?" asked Sæwald skeptically.

"Yes, yes. Virgin? No man."

Brimhild didn't follow this facet of Gobban's religion. Sæwald laughed incredulously. "A virgin? Oh, no!"

Gobban did not smile at Sæwald's merriment. "Is true."

Hildilid was torn. The priest was clearly dreaming, yet he was her guest. "She had a baby?"

"Yes. Son God."

"What happened to this son God. Jesus, you say?"

"Yes. He grow up. Man. Good man. Help people. They sick, he doctor. They lost, he find. He good man."

"What happened to him?" asked Brimhild eagerly.

"He killed. He die. Bad men kill him."

"Why didn't his father stop it? Wasn't the father God there? Couldn't he stop the death?" asked Sæwald.

"Father God there. No help. Can no help."

"Then he's no god. A god has power."

"Even Odin will be consumed by Fenrir the wolf when the end comes. And he was hung in a tree when he learned the runes," pointed out Hildilid.

"Hang in tree! Yes, yes, son God hang in tree too. Then die."

"So your one God is dead."

"No, no. Son God live again. Three days pass, he live again."

Sæwald was utterly contemptuous, for all his fondness of Gobban. "How could a dead thing live again?"

"When Baldr was killed by the mistletoe, the gods were told he could live again if all creation wept." Hildilid did think Gobban's faith a bit odd. Yet there were some far-fetched parallels to her own.

"All creation did not weep, did it?" said Sæwald cynically.

"Yet after Ragnarök Baldr is to rule. The destruction of the world will give rise to peace and Odin's son." Hildilid mused to herself that there was perhaps something to the stranger's lore.

"Where does the son God live?" asked Brimhild.

"He live here. Everywhere. We eat and drink him."

Here he really lost his audience. "Eat and drink?" asked Hildilid. By now Sæwald did not even bother to try to comprehend.

"Yes, yes. We speak, special words. Son God live in wine and bread."

"I do like those," agreed Sæwald, "but I never ran across a bone or spit from a god!"

"We drink wine. That son God blood. We eat bread. That son God body."

"So you are nothing more than cannibals!" said Sæwald. Hildilid shushed him.

Brimhild asked, "How can you eat your god? Don't you love him?"

"Yes, yes, love. Eat, drink, love. We eat love, we drink love."

The entire family was rather confused. Granted, the language impasse did not help. And it did strike them as barbaric to eat one's own god. They didn't even accuse their worst enemies, the Heathobards, of such an atrocity.

"Tell me about the mother of the son God," asked Brimhild.

"Good mother. Help baby. No place to have baby. Looking, looking. Find barn with animals. Have baby with animals."

"Isn't he the son of the father God? Why was he not born in the meadhall, like the children of kings?" asked Sæwald.

"Yes, son God son of father God. No money. No gold. Poor boy."

Sæwald said, "Our gods live in a splendid hall of gold and glory."

"Our son God not king like Scylding king. No meadhall. No

gold."

"Why would anyone chose to worship such a pitiful god?"

"Perhaps because he is so pitiful, Daddy," said Brimhild, her eyes glittering with tears for the poor boy. She had been poor and lost. Such a boy she could love. Though she respected Odin, she could not love him.

"Pity is no strong feeling, child," warned Sæwald. "Pity weakens those who feel it. It is best to think of your family honor. Therein lies strength."

"How, Daddy?"

"Let me tell you a story. Not of cannibals and weakling gods. Of strong men and women here in middle earth." Brimhild climbed into his lap. She gave Gobban a quick look, to let him know she shared with him a softness for the low son god. Sæwald began his story.

"You know that Odin and Loki are gods. Odin is the All-Father, god of battle, inspiration, and death. He is a worthy Æsir, the family of gods who rule us. Loki was the son of a giant. He was very beautiful to gaze upon. That helped him to be powerful. He was no trustworthy god. He did evil deeds. He disliked peace. For this, he is much hated.

"Odin and Loki were not always enemies. This takes place before Loki had Odin's beloved son, Baldr, killed. They passed along the world and one day saw an otter beside a waterfall. He was filling up on salmon and was tired in the haze of the sun. His eyes were half shut. He did not notice the gods. He did not see Loki pick up a stone and throw it. Then that beast lay dead. Odin and Loki ate both animal and fish. For that, Loki was proud.

"That night the gods stopped at the house of a man named Hreidmar. He worried about his son who had not come home with his brothers, Fafnir and Regin. Loki and Odin said they did not see that missing boy when they ate the otter at the waterfall. Hreidmar hardened his face. 'You ate an otter?' 'Yes,' said Loki, cheerfully, 'was that not a good shot? To get both otter and salmon in one shot.' The brothers and father surrounded the gods. 'You have come to the right home,' said Hreidmar, 'for that otter was my son in disguise.'

"The gods knew they would be killed if they did not do as Hreidmar demanded. They had to fill the otter skin up with gold, then cover that precious skin with gold until it could be seen no more.

"Where could the gods find sufficient gold? Loki remembered that a dwarf, named Andvari, hoarded gold. 'If we find that ugly creature,' said Loki, 'we can take his treasure. For who suits gold and luxury best? A shrunken brute or a shining god?' Odin agreed and they sought out Andvari, who had transformed himself into a fish. Loki leaped into the mountain pool and the slippery thing escaped the god's grasp. Ultimately, no low being can avoid a god completely. Andvari turned back into his wretched self and demanded to know what Loki was seeking. 'I need your gold hoard. There's been an accident. Hreidmar requires it.' 'Why should I help?' squealed the dwarf. 'Let me go!' 'Only once you've given me your gold.' Andvari sighed. He knew he'd have to give up the hoard.

"They went to his cave. In it were piled glittering treasures and gleaming swords, shining jewels and bright booty. 'There. Take it and leave me be!' Odin and Loki poured the treasures into the otter skin, filling several bags with the shining stuff to place over the fur coat. All the gold disappeared. Now the cave was dingy and dim.

"Odin and Loki started off. As they left, Andvari cried out, 'Don't ever come back!' Loki turned around and noticed the swiftest glimpse of a shining gleam. 'What's that?' asked Loki, approaching the little man. 'Nothing! Go away! Leave me be!' screamed Andvari as the god grasped his arm and a ring fell out onto the earth below. Odin bent over and picked it up. 'No! No! Take anything but that!' The misshapen wretch was desperate. Now the gods were intrigued.

"'And why do you want that ring so eagerly? It couldn't be magic, could it?' taunted Loki. Andvari cried, 'It will help me become rich again. It is cursed for all others. Whoever possesses it will know destruction. Return the ring to me, or doom shall prevail.' The dwarf was in despair. Hot tears ran down his scruffy beard. He was a hideous sight to the shining gods who refused to believe him. 'We'll take our chances,' said Odin. As it turned out, the gods needed that ring. The booty covered the otter skin completely, save for one whisker which stuck out. The ring lay over it, a fateful shelter.

"That decayed rascal, Andvari, was no liar. Hreidmar, the grieving father, was killed by his own sons for the bewitching gold. Fafnir turned himself into a dragon and made his home upon the gold. That was no cozy hearth. Regin, the fireworm's brother, lured the hero, Sigurd, to kill that fever snake. Sigurd savored that serpent's warm blood and understood the birds. They warned him of Regin's treachery. Sigurd killed the last of the brothers, saving himself for the doom the ring promised. That is another story."

Brimhild stared into the fire, imagining it snorting from the nostrils of that fever snake, Fafnir. Such a story, terrifying and wonderful, thrilled her young ears.

Gobban spoke. "No good story. Bad gods. Bad men. No kill brother."

"Well," hazarded Sæwald, "the brothers were bad to kill each other and their father. They needed to have gold to recompense their first brother's death. In our society we call that wergild. You pay for your misdeeds with money. Then no bloodshed ensues."

"Much blood in story. No good. Better do like son God say." Gobban did not know how to express it. He turned his face to the side.

Hildilid, Sæwald, and Brimhild tried to guess what he meant. "Turn to the side? Turn away?" At this, Gobban excitedly nodded his head. "Turn away?"

"When bad man come, he do bad thing. No kill bad man. Turn away. What this called?" Gobban pointed to the space between his nose and his ear.

"Cheek," said Brimhild.

Gobban pretended to hit his right cheek. "You hit here. Then I say," Gobban turned to show his left cheek, "please hit here."

Hildilid said, "You mean, you want to be hit?"

"Turn aside cheek. Turn away cheek. No get angry. Son God Jesus say turn aside cheek."

Brimhild tried to imagine what Gobban meant. It seemed that he urged not avenging a death, nor even asking for wergild — simply to turn away and carry on with one's life. That would be impossible! Could there be such a world, where people did not get angry at misdeeds, and simply forgot them? He even seemed to think that if you got hurt, you should ask to be hurt more. It made no sense.

"No forget bad thing. Say sorry, excuse."

Sæwald laughed. "You mean, if you killed my father, I'm just supposed to say, that's alright, let's forget about this. I'll just carry on. Don't even give me compensation?" He was utterly incredulous.

"Yes, yes. Turn aside," Gobban pointed to his face, "cheek. I say sorry, sorry, excuse."

"You'd have to do a lot more than that if you killed my father!"

Hildilid stood up, fearful that Sæwald was taking this all a bit too seriously. It was obvious that Gobban's religion was so peculiar it would never go far. "More to drink?" she asked warmly, hoping they could move on to another subject.

Sæwald's cruel and playful gods were reminiscent of those Roman gods now losing their power, so Gobban told them about Jupiter and Juno. These tales pleased Sæwald more than the Christian ones and their naughiness delighted Brimhild.

"Mama," said Brimhild one day, "do you think my family put me to sea so I would not be killed?"

"Why do you ask that now, darling?"

"Because, Gobban says it's better to not kill. Maybe someone put me to sea so I would not be killed for some reason. I think they must have wanted to save me."

"Of course, they did. They left you with food and drink and—" Hildilid stopped. She planned to tell Brimhild about her golden treasures when she was older.

"And what, Mama?"

"And blankets to keep you warm."

"Do you think those people wanted to turn aside the cheek? You know, what Gobban is talking about."

"I don't know, darling."

"Of course not," shouted Sæwald. "Those people were in pretty desperate straits, let me tell you. Naturally they wanted you to live. It had nothing to do with cheeks or this silly nonsense Gobban babbles about."

And that was that.

Nonetheless, Brimhild thought, every so often, about what she would do if someone hit her on the right cheek. Would she call her father, tell him what happened, and have her injury avenged? Or would she present her left cheek to the offender and say, "Please, hit me again. I will excuse you?" It seemed a strange world where people willingly agreed to be hurt. Though she had to admit that many people got hurt when revenge governed their lives.

Gobban stayed with them several more weeks. His language skills improved and they heard more about the father God and the son God. It still seemed silly to them to eat a god already dead. Or was he living again? No, no, it was against logic. They supplied Gobban with warm clothes, food, water gourds and a small and sturdy boat. He waved as he sailed off.

"I hope his son god can save him from the Jutes and Heathobards."

"Sæwald," hissed Hildilid, motioning that Brimhild was

listening.

"Will he live?" the child asked.

"He'll live again," said Sæwald, meaning it sarcastically. Yet the girl took hope in that sentiment. Perhaps, like that son God, he will live again. She pitied Gobban for his sorry and shabby god. Much better to have one who can battle giants and chant spells. Still, she felt haunted by the image of the little son God born among the animals, spurned by the mead hall drinkers with their golden cups, and tended to by the clean mother who had known no man.

Chapter 4

Leech Lore

As Brimhild was growing up, she would visit her aunt in her hut by the murky mere. Smaller than her parents' home, it had a hearth and chimney at one end. Its walls were of wattle and daub and a roof made of turf from the peat Ælfsciene cut from aside the mere. A goat peeked its head out from its stall the first time the girl came to spend the night. The whole house smelled of peat, straw, and animal ordure. Yet a sweeter scent pierced Brimhild's senses too, a kind of incense from the many flowers and plants that her aunt gathered.

Ælfsciene taught her the wisdom of women, magic medicine. Herbs could heal, plants could improve, worts could make well. Sometimes Brimhild would visit Auntie's hut, hugging the mere, to learn leech lore, crafty cures. "This knowledge has been known for many hundred half-years, passed down from mother, womb-wise woman, to daughter, avid apprentice. Learn these things well, Brimhild, one may save the life of a loved one. One flower may fashion a favorable physic. That spell could spin succor, that recipe relieve."

At these times, Aunt Ælfsciene would tell stories of the past to Brimhild.

"The warrior Sigurd, valiant Volsung, sought out the shield-maiden ringed by fire. This was after he killed the dragon, got gold, spoke with sparrows. Flames did not burn him, heat did not hate him. There lay a warrior, helmeted hero. Sigurd removed that hat, winning more gold, glinting off tresses. That warrior was a maiden, Brynhild by name. She taught him rune lore, gave him good counsel. They pledged their faith, promised their love.

"Then Sigurd drank, a foamy forgetting. That was Grimhild's

glass. Her daughter, Gudrun, loved that fighter. Sigurd married that woman, Grimhild's daughter, Gunnar's sister, Brynhild's foe.

"Gunnar sought Brynhild, desired Valkyrie. Brynhild would marry only that man who could walk through flames, fight with fire. Sigurd helped Gunnar. With magical means, Sigurd, in Gunnar's guise, reached the fell female. Brynhild was no happy bride, joined to Gunnar. Her heart belonged to the Volsung.

"Gudrun mocked Brynhild, praised Sigurd, her own stout-hearted spouse. Brynhild spoke hotly. No woman can keep two husbands and the peace. She bid Gunnar kill her true love. After Sigurd's doom, she pierced her breast, foresaw ill fortune, begged to be burned with that hero's corpse. She died, happy her ashes would mingle with his. Brynhild was no frightened female, winsome wife. That maiden's memory remains with us."

Brimhild was silent after hearing of Brynhild's death. Then she asked her aunt, "What happened to Gudrun?"

"She married twice more. Not to men of her choosing." Ælfsciene looked at Brimhild. "I will tell you her story one day. Listen now, girl." The crone picked up a blossoming herb. "Do you see this?" Brimhild nodded. "If I keep it as it is, it smells lovely. Nothing more. It remains inactive. If I add it to betony, it heals. If I add it to this flower, it poisons." Brimhild concentrated, realizing her aunt was determined to teach her something beyond leechlore. "Brimhild, promise me that in your life you will not be inert. Don't poison yourself within. The path your life takes should be a creating way, not a destroying way. I believe you arrived on these shores for a reason. Heal yourself and this land."

"How?" Ælfsciene's lesson was like the ebb tide, freezing her toes that drew back, only to have the chill moisture touch her again and slip away.

"Find the man you love and marry him. If you can't find such a man, find a life you love and lead it. That's what I have done."

Brimhild held her aunt's hand. "Why have you never married, Auntie? Did you never love?"

"I loved," she said grimly. "The man I loved was hated. I watched his foes split open his belly before I could put my body between my lover and the sword. I heal others, since I could not heal him."

"I am sorry, Auntie."

"That was many years ago. Now I am almost dead." She paused. "I have healed many bodies, others withered and decayed." Brimhild bowed her head in silent contemplation. Ælfsciene looked at the solemn maid. "Shall I tell you of other fates?"

"Oh, yes, please, Auntie," said Brimhild eagerly.

The old woman recounted. "Hrothgar's great-grandfather was Scyld Scefing."

"I heard, Auntie, that he was a great warrior."

"He was a great killer, which is no surprise seeing as he was the son of a drab and a drunken lay-about. He killed the true king and set himself up as a bully of the people. Then he slaughtered and raped his way across the sea."

"What is raped, Auntie?"

"He took women's honor. And with it his own honor."

"Why would he do that, Auntie?"

"It has been the custom for the new king to go on a rampage after he is chosen. That is to show how worthy he is to be king. By killing and disrespecting life and honor, he fills himself with honor and worth. It's a family tradition." Ælfsciene was scornful, disdainful dame. "Hrothgar was only thirty half-years when he became king and went on many a furtive journey abroad. He proved himself worthy of that throne."

"Auntie, it does not sound like pleasant work."

"It isn't, girl. It is better to fish in your own sea and be cleansed by the salt water of the teeming waves, than to create trouble for yourself."

"Auntie, surely the court is no longer like that. I mean, these raiding parties are no longer so acceptable, are they?"

"I fear they'll never go out of favor. Not so long as ambition rules men's hearts and blood lust flows in their veins."

Brimhild did not understand. She could sense that the court was not a perfect place, yet everyone talked about it as though it were the center of their lives. Its importance meant to her that it had to have some worth, even if the glory was imaginary, at best ephemeral.

Her mother, having been brought up at court and heartened by the king's request to bring Brimhild there when she was older, taught the child the ways of court. Not to mince or be soft, but the strong things that could be imparted from such knowledge. Hildilid told how the queen would carry the cup from the king to his rival, from whatever tribe was conquered or treatied with. The queen wove a web of peace in the carrying of the cup from man to man, retainer to retainer. Her symbolic act meant more than the meaningless promises of faith. Yet even that web could be tangled by treachery, the swearing of deceitful oaths.

The hall, Hildilid told her, was large and wooden, solid and heavy. There were tables and benches to eat at and even sleep on. The floor was covered with straw which would be replaced by the men every week or so. The retainers slept on the floors, tables, and benches of the main hall and were responsible for maintaining it. Some retainers were grown men with families. They would visit periodically, tending their own farms or fishing one to three days' journey hence. They would come to offer counsel throughout the year, sometimes leaving the farm in the hands of a son or wife, other times travelling with a companion, close comrade. Sons they brought to the hall when they were twelve or thirteen, to introduce them to court life. The boys loved it, of course. Playing and fighting with one another, grabbing a kiss from a girl, it was a place of mischief and learning. If a man had several sons, he would often spare the most incompetent farmer for the court. Hildilid's father had allowed her brother Scyldtheow to be a shore guard to strengthen the ties between family and king.

Females were no less valuable, helping their mothers milk the cows, feed the animals, sew, cook, and clean on the farm. A large family might send a spare girl to learn the courtly ways and wed a retainer. In a sense, the king was surrounded by the least-favored offspring of his people, who were greedy to keep the cream of the crop for themselves. Hildilid had been sent to the court at thirteen as she was the fourth girl to be born in the family. Though of high favor, the court woman's life was, in actuality, one of drudgery. The women lived in an adjacent hall to the men, containing stalls with curtains creating little privacy or warmth. The women came and went from the main hall, keeping their own residence pristeen. The king's compound, in addition to the two main buildings, had numerous outbuildings. It was, in effect, a very large farm. So the courtiers and ladies, in addition to their chores of cooking and cleaning, had to take care of the animals too.

Was there no one of a lower birth who could tend to these activities? As virtually all farmed to survive, there was little opportunity for the society to have developed a hierarchy of privilege. It is true—there were the inevitable shiftless members, that every society knows—beggars, drunkards, and loose ladies. If some poor farmer's family was on the brink of disaster, he might send his children to the court to be servants. They tended to marry among themselves, creating a servant class, though a pretty girl could marry a witless retainer if he were not paying attention. Existence was eked out day by day. Even the king had been seen to muck out the stables.

Things were changing, Hildilid told Brimhild. A new time was coming. She heard that the retainers and court ladies did less physical labor now that sufficient servants were at court. Success brought slaves, captured concubines, persecuted prisoners, humbled heathens. This freed the ladies to concentrate on fine sewing, even the fashioning of jeweled ornaments to adorn their bodies.

Brimhild would pretend she was the peaceweaver. Holding a mug carved of wood, she would hand it from doll to doll, shell to seaweed, pretending she was the queen who laced her people in peace.

After Brimhild had been with them thirty half-years, Hildilid wanted her taken to the court to be trained in court ways. "At home you only see us, Brimhild."

"I only want to see you."

"You need to meet other people, darling. You will learn the ways of the retainers and the ladies of the court. One day you will marry. There are no young men here. I married for love and I wish for you to do so as well."

"What if that man is not at court?"

"Then we will need to look beyond the sea."

"How? Where?"

Her mother would not answer.

Sæwald took Brimhild to the hall. Along the way they spent the night at Ælfsciene's hut by the mere. Ælfsciene was against the decision to place Brimhild at court.

"She need only to stay as long as she wishes, Auntie," Sæwald said in defense of their decision. "What else is she to do? Fish with me until I die? Then what would be her fate?"

"I am alone," said Ælfsciene, "and happy for it."

"And so are all your potential suitors," he teased.

Auntie laughed. "Listen to me, girl," she said seriously, "always follow your heart. At court it is easy to follow envy or greed. That will leave you with nothing. Obey your deepest desire and you cannot go wrong."

"Truly, Auntie?"

"If you do, at least it will be of your own doing, so you cannot reproach anyone else. That is the worst worm, regret."

Chapter 5

Red Gold

The following day the girl saw the hall for the first time. Her father pointed it out, clinging on a gentle slope. It sat among a series of low buildings against the horizon. They looked ragged and sloppy, stretched out haphazardly.

"Where is the golden hall?" asked Brimhild.

Her father laughed. "Only in tales do halls have gilt walls. Hrothgar has added on building after building here as his success has increased. It's truly remarkable."

Sæwald no longer saw the buildings for what they were— miserable shacks. It is true that the main hall was a large rectangular structure. At one time the animals had had their stalls at one end, as in most homes. Recently a byre had been built just for them. The main hall had a hearth built on a clay foundation at one end. Heavy posts supported the weight of the roof.

Sæwald led her to the women's quarters, housed in a building fashioned in the old manner, with stalls at one end.

Brimhild hugged her father tightly goodbye. "If you need us, Brimhild," he said, "we will come." So promised her father.

Brimhild's training as a lady consisted of slopping out the hogs, milking cows, and washing clothes, much as she had at home. The only difference between this life and the life with her parents was that here she worked, lonely, before the sun rose until long after it dipped below the shimmering horizon. The worst was being separated from her family, loving parents. She wondered if this were the glorious court life sung of in lays.

Brimhild was mocked sometimes for her rusticity, how she loved to walk in the chill breeze and gaze at the horizon, hoping for a glimpse of her father's boat. She made friends with the slaves—low laborers, miserable men, wretched women, chilled children. This the hall maidens could not understand—how Brimhild felt akin to those wronged workers. Though she had parents, like the dolorous captives she had been born abroad, mysterious maiden. They spoke different tongues, all struggled with Scylding speech, Danish dialect. Brimhild's language, too, was foreign, lyrical, magical, distant from the gable-gabble.

One day some court girls were fooling in the kitchen. They acted out the ceremony of handing around the cup of peace. They made believe that they first handed the cup to the warriors, weak with wine. Brimhild stopped them, saying, "You're doing it all wrong." She showed them how to do it as in the old manner. She bore the studded cup to an imaginary king, then to the trustworthy thanes, reliable retainers. The girl, pretending princess, then drank from the gold goblet herself, made words of welcome. She was a good queen!

The girls complained to Hrothgar's mother who came to the kitchens to see who had caused the uproar. She knew who Brimhild was.

"I saw you shortly after you washed ashore, like a piece of driftwood or seaweed." The girls giggled and Brimhild turned red. "But," continued the queen, in a tone that hushed the giggly girls, "you know the old ways of diplomacy better than these silly sheep. It is good to pluck treasure from the sea when it profits you."

After that the girls no longer mocked her to her face. They acted warily in her presence.

One of the slave girls came up to Brimhild later that night.

"Excuse me, miss."

Brimhild turned around from the pile of mead-horns she was washing. "Yes." She knew the girl was a slave from the collar around her neck. No burnished torque, this was a heavy reminder of servitude, firm fetter.

"I heard those girls this afternoon with you. You showed them, didn't you, miss?"

"Please don't call me 'miss.' My name is Brimhild. What is yours?"

"I'm Helga. I just wanted to say, Brimhild"–Helga blushed as she said the name–"that I thought you showed true honor. Those foolish girls know nothing of the proper way of ceremony, its solemnity, its gravity."

"My mother taught me how to weave the peace ring when I was a child. I practiced many times with my dolls."

Helga laughed. "I also did!" Remembering her present state, she became grave.

Brimhild continued washing the cups and Helga swept. Finally, Brimhild asked, "Where do you come from, Helga?"

"I come from the north and west of here. I'm a Jute. Or, at least, I was. Now the Scyldings hold sway over my birth land. We are dispossessed."

Brimhild looked at her earnestly. "I'm sorry."

Ealhhild, the queen mother, came in while the girls were talking. "Now, now, Brimhild, you have a lot of work to do. Stop chattering and get back to your duties. There's time enough for chit-chat when the kitchen is clean."

"Of course," whispered Helga, as Ealhhild left, "the warriors," and at that she rolled her eyes, "drink all night so there's never any end to the kitchen work. We always have to clean up after the likes of them. If not their cups, then their vomit."

Brimhild laughed. Helga looked to be about two winters older than herself. And had spent how many years in captivity? Of course, it didn't seem much different from her own life. After all, she had to clean and obey orders, too, to gain a place in the mead-hall and win a husband from among the drunken warriors.

A few days later, Brimhild was told to fetch a cow and her calf from a neighboring farm to bring back to the king's settlement. Ealhhild was giving her instructions and Brimhild noticed Helga pass by.

"Can I bring one of the slaves with me to help?" she asked.

"I suppose so," agreed Ealhhild. Brimhild hurried to tell Helga.

The two young women headed off, carrying ropes with which to tie the animals.

"I'm glad you asked if I could accompany you," said Helga, a little shyly.

"Oh, I wanted your company. You seem so nice and level-headed. Those other girls, well, they just flirt with the boys and fool in the hall. I like to have fun too. But they seem a little mean." She reflected back on the cruel remarks she had sometimes heard the girls make about the slaves being sluts. Helga did not seem like that at all. She certainly didn't carry on with the men the way those goosey maids did.

They walked in silence for a while, taking in the view from the hilltop where the hall estate was placed. From that summit, you could look over the bay towards the rugged mainland to the west, or to the east over the sea. The sea was dazzlingly blue as they headed down the slope to a farm a few miles distant.

"Where do you come from?" asked Helga.

"I don't know," answered Brimhild, simply.

"You don't know?" Helga was incredulous.

"Well, of course, I have a mother and father here. They're Scyldings. I was a foundling."

"Oh." Helga didn't know what to say. Should she say she was sorry?

"I adore my parents. It's just that I came from the sea."

"The sea?"

"I arrived in a little boat when I was a child, a toddler. I don't remember anything about my life before that. I just wish I knew what happened to my people." She stopped to look at the white caps glinting the sun's light. "I hope they are still alive." She held a hand over her forehead to keep off the brightness. It made her eyes tear.

Helga halted with her. "I hope mine are, as well."

Brimhild came out of her reverie. "I'm sorry. How stupid of me. Of course. Your people, well, they are slaves, too?"

"I don't know." Helga began to walk. At first she said nothing. Then she began to speak. She couldn't stop.

"I come from a fishing village northwest of here. My father had a farm and fished in the sea. He sometimes was counselor to our king. My mother and sister and I ran the farm when he had to go to the hall to aid the king. One day, only about two years ago now, the Scyldings landed. They pulled their longships up the shore. The prows made an awful noise scraping against the shale. There were too many boats at once for it to be fishermen. We looked up from our front garden. We had been weeding. My father quickly went inside and got a sword. He ordered us to run into the hills and not come out again until he called for us. My mother, sister Inga, and I ran away from the beach. There was a cave in the hills we could hide in. The animals were kept there in winter.

"We ran as fast as we could go. Inga was only seven, and so we had to slow our pace to stay with her. My mother told me to go ahead, they would catch up with me. I refused. If they died, I wanted to die too. I don't think death was what my mother feared for me. I was fifteen, old enough to be dishonored.

"They caught my mother. Two Scyldings held her down. I beat them and one stood up and pulled me back while the other—"

Helga was crying. Brimhild put her arms around her. After a moment, Helga burst out. "I didn't care about me! I only wanted to save my mother and Inga!"

Brimhild murmered how she was sure that was true.

"You don't see! That second fighter took me, as the first slit my mother's throat." Helga continued, speaking lowly now. "I didn't care about me. I only cared about saving Inga."

"What happened to her?"

"When that first Scylding cut my mother's neck, her beaded string fell off. He picked up what beads he could. I could see, as the second man dirtied me, two little beads roll away, hidden in the grass. I memorized that spot. I stared at that spot as he grunted away, praying those beads would remain hidden from their evil glance.

"He finished at last. 'You're a good girl,' he said, and turned to burn our houses. Inga sat by a tree, collapsed, her knees up to her chins, shaking, unable to cry or speak. 'Inga, Inga, I'm all right,' I lied, the blood streaming down my legs, just as it dripped below my mother's white face. I ran to the beads, picked them up, and thrust one into Inga's hand. She clutched it senselessly.

"'Keep this always, Inga. These two beads are for us, they are from Mommy. No matter what happens, I will always remember you, I will always try to find you, I will always know you.' I heard the men returning. 'Swallow it. Swallow it!' I shouted at her. My poor sister swallowed the bead, choking and coughing. It went down, just as it went down my unsevered throat. 'When it comes out, swallow it again. Keep on swallowing it until one day, when it is safe, you can make a necklace of it. Hide it against your heart. That bead is me, the one I have swallowed is you. We will always be together this way. I will always have you in me. I don't care if it takes thirty years, we will be together. We will not be separated.'

"Then the men came, the glorious warriors, the honorable thanes." Helga snorted in disgust. "They were noble fighters! Then they took us to their boats, Inga and I chained together along with other people from the village. That night I slept with my arms just touching Inga. The chains were too short to let me embrace her. She still shook in terror. I sang to her and muttered half-words all night. She fell asleep at last.

"When morning came, the fetters were removed. Oh, I wish that they had stayed on! For with that freedom came the loss of my sister. She was taken to another Scylding vessel with other young children. I shouted to her, 'Never forget! I shall never forget!' The last I saw of her was through the flood's fury, the wave's water. I know not where she was taken. I was hustled into a longship with the older girls and young women. They brought us here. Some have stayed, others have moved on. I have not found out where she is."

"Did you see the men again who manned her ship? Won't any of the Scylding men tell you where they took her?"

"I know who manned it. He says he doesn't know where she could be. By now, it could be anywhere. She must have been sold."

The wind died down. They heard the birds calling and the insects hum. They walked on to the farm, in silence.

"Do you have it still?" asked Brimhild.

"Have what?"

"The bead."

Helga pulled aside the neck of her dress. A scratchy piece of twine lay around her neck. It had rubbed into her skin, making it red and sore. By her breast lay a small yellowish bead made of amber. Brimhild reached up her hand, and held it like a talisman. It shone in the sun.

Helga sang a slave's song, lament for liberty.

I wake
when the moon
still shines on the white-peaked waves.
Sometimes I think that instead of
stoking the fire,
boiling the clothes,
killing the lamb,
tending every want,
suffering every shame,
I'll walk into that water
until I reach my home

across the seas.

Back at the hall, Brimhild shared a bed with three other girls. When she and Helga returned from the farm, she asked Ealhhild if she could share a bed with Helga instead. "Please, lady, she is a sweet girl. I know she is a slave. Let me be her friend. Those other girls taunt me. It makes me unhappy."

Ealhhild sighed. "You like her because she came from over the sea like you. You shouldn't pity her, even though you pity yourself."

"I don't pity myself!"

"You do! You think yourself too good for the court. You are too pure for such a place. Yes, the other girls are silly, but they are not slaves. Helga is. Yet, she is a hard-worker. You may be her companion. Only if it will not hinder your work. You're here to see how a hall is run. All you girls are, to see if you're up to the life of the meadhall. You may go with her. I'll warn you—her bed is already crowded with three other slaves. I know that Helga is a good girl."

That's just what Helga's attacker had said to her after—. Brimhild tried not to think of that and went to tell Helga the good news.

After this they were inseparable. Brimhild didn't mind taking on lower chores left to the slaves, just so she and her friend could be together and not be lonely.

One night, not long after she moved into Helga's room, she woke up. She could hear the heavy snores of one of the other slaves, and the deep breathing of the other girls. She saw a white flash leave their stall. Helga was missing! It must have been her.

It was odd. After all, they had a pot to pee in during the night if it were necessary. Brimhild lay there, unable to sleep. Two hours later Helga returned. Brimhild whispered, "Where have you been?"

Helga gasped. "How long have you been awake?"

"I saw you go."

"What else did you see?" Helga seemed angry.

"Nothing. What's wrong? Are you ill?"

"I'm fine! Just leave me alone!" Helga turned away from Brimhild and pretended to sleep. Brimhild couldn't understand how she had angered Helga. She had wanted to help her.

The next few days were tense. Brimhild didn't want to bring up what had happened to Helga, and Helga seemed determined not to explain.

Then, one night, the same thing happened. They had lain in bed for about an hour, when Helga got up. This time Brimhild followed her. She wrapped a dark cloak around her to keep warm and to hide her white gown from the night. Helga didn't bother with cloaks. She shone like a candle.

Brimhild saw something dark reach out and Helga disappear. Brimhild sucked in her breath. She stopped and crept forward. Ahead were some of the animals' stalls. She walked inch by inch, slowly making her way. Then she came to the first stall and looked in.

Though there were no horses or cows there, Brimhild saw animals. Human animals. She could see Helga's face beneath the long hair of the man crouched over her. Her dress had been yanked up over her hips. Tears gleamed on the slave's cheeks. She lay inert. Then the man finished. "You're a good girl, Helga." He turned over. It was Unferth, Hrothgar's head advisor.

"May I go?" asked Helga.

"No, let's talk. Why won't you be nice to me?" asked Unferth playfully.

"Be nice to you? What do you call this?"

"I don't think you fancy me."

"Why should I?"

At that Unferth hit her across the cheek.

Brimhild gasped.

"Who's there?" shouted Unferth. Brimhild ran back to the bed. Her dark cloak concealed her from the sage counsellor.

Helga came back to bed half an hour later. She curled up at the edge of the bed. Brimhild saw her shoulders shaking as Helga, sobbing, sucked in great gasps of air.

The next day Brimhild confronted Helga. "You must tell someone. You must tell the queen mother. This should not continue."

"You don't understand, Brimhild. You are so innocent. Have you forgotten? I'm a slave. I am property. Anything can be done to me. Just like they might kick a chair or burn down a house, they can do what they like with me."

"I refuse to believe it!"

"Brimhild, don't you do anything foolish! I can bear this. If you make waves, then who knows what would happen to me."

"I can't let you be raped like this, again and again."

"And again. Don't you think it torments me? Yet if you tell, they may see me as trouble. I could be killed."

Brimhild couldn't stand it. Night after night, Helga would go, returning shaking with misery. Finally, Helga was showing the child she would bear.

"See," said Wulfrun, one of the apprentices like Brimhild, "those slaves are so wanton! She probably had it off with another slave in the privy!"

Brimhild turned on Wulfrun in fury. "How dare you speak about Helga that way! Or any slave? Do you know what she has gone through? What those stalwart soldiers in the hall are capable of? Those warriors you flirt with, flashing your ankle, promising comfort, take out their arousal on slaves just like her."

"They wouldn't lower themselves to touch filth like that."

"You are the wanton one, you are the slut. For your laugh kindles the image of your open thighs in their depraved minds."

Wulfrun jumped on Brimhild, scratching her nails deep into her face, drawing hot red. Brimhild battled with her, just as Ealhhild entered at the tumult.

"What do you two think you're doing?" thundered Ealhhild.

The sound of her voice caused the girls to stop their violence. Their chests were heaving. Complete silence reigned. All Brimhild could hear was her blood thundering, pounding in her ears. She could see Helga had come in. How much had she heard?

"Well, Brimhild, you are always one for saying these girls are low. Now you are marked with their folly. So is Wulfrun." Ealhhild motioned to Wulfrun's bruised face.

"Yes, you are right, lady. I have lowered myself to their level. I was sorely provoked."

"I'm sure you were." Ealhhild looked closely at Brimhild. Then she clapped her hands. "All of you leave. I wish to speak to Brimhild alone." Wulfrun smirked. "I will deal with you later," Ealhhild promised Wulfrun. And she did.

"Can you explain this, Brimhild?" asked Ealhhild. "I could see you didn't want to talk in front of the other girls. What's been going on?"

"I cannot say, lady. I have been sworn to secrecy."

"Surely you can hint, Brimhild. Does it have something to do with Helga?"

"Yes, lady. I worry for her. Wulfrun said terrible things about her. It's awfully low to mock a slave, a person who can't defend herself. It's horrid to harm any defenseless being."

"You are living in the wrong land, then, Brimhild. You know we are not a gentle folk. We cannot be. Everyone has slaves. Such is life. Slaves are well treated here. I have always prided myself on that."

"Are they well treated, lady?"

"What do you mean?"

"I cannot say, lady. I only wonder how Helga got pregnant. I can tell you no slave is the father of that child."

Ealhhild reddened. "What do you imply?"

"I say nothing. Only what other men are here?"

"The warriors have their needs."

"Do they? Do they include terrorizing helpless women?"

"Listen, girl. There is a riddle. 'I am a sorry worm. I shrivel when ice cold. See me in the heat of battle, then I am a shining blade.' Do you know the answer?"

"I can guess."

"Then let the warriors do their work. They keep you safe."

"By making others unsafe."

"Girl, girl, you are so naive. You know so little, for all your wisdom of the old ceremonies. Grow up, little miss, or you will never be happy here."

"I fear I shall not be."

"Return to your parents. You can be a fisherman's wife."

"I promised my parents I would stay and give it a try. I owe it to them to fulfill my vow. I am no oath-breaker."

"That is good. I think you are sturdy within, Brimhild, for all your sentimental talk. Just remember. You can't have high ceremony without bloodshed. Why do you think they call it 'red gold'? Because each brooch which gleams from our breasts was sprinkled in blood, scarlet sap, each cup of golden honey mead has a drop of blood, crimson claret, in it." Ealhhild swung her skirt around, and left the kitchen. "Now, you!" Brimhild could hear the queen mother shout at Wulfrun.

After this incident, there was no more trouble from Wulfrun.

Chapter 6

The Flaxen Foe

After several months of drudgery, Brimhild was released to higher activites. During her apprenticeship, she was diligent. However, she didn't like the court and yearned for the sea. To evoke the past, she sang the eerie tunes her father and mother had lulled to her, haunting melodies Auntie Ælfsciene had crooned.

One day, while she was piling seaweed on the shore, she sang of her lost family.

A hooded man stood listening. Brimhild had not noticed him. She stopped her mouth when he walked up to her.

"Do you sing, maid?"

"Yes. I sing to entertain the fish and crabs."

"It is a pretty melody."

"I learned it in the sea."

"Are you a mermaid? For I have heard tell of women, half-human, half-fish. Or perhaps a Valkyrie? They are flying warriors, sleek like swans. Remember how Weland, blacksmith to the gods, came upon the three sisters spinning flax. Beside them lay their swanskins, aerial armor. Weland and his brothers stole those clothes, Valkyrie veils. So Weland won Hervor the Allwise."

"She never lost her longing to join those warrior women. Finally he lost her. I may be a Valkyrie. Or perhaps, mead-maddened, you only dream," Brimhild saucily replied, raking weed all the while. She continued to sing and work. As the man walked away, he drew his hood back to listen better. It was Hrothgar, king of the Scyldings, lord of the Ingwines. Later, his kinship to Weland would be made known.

He asked his mother who the girl was. Ealhhild explained it

was the same maid who had washed ashore years ago. "And now she teaches the silly girls in the kitchen ceremonies in the old manner."

The king was intrigued and desired to see her more.

At twilight he stirred again on the shore. He saw her shock of red-gold hair, glowing in the gloam, streaming behind her in the strong breeze. This time Brimhild saw him approach.

"The king seeks fresh winds to clear his thoughts."

"No, I yearn for perfumed breezes to fog my senses."

"Then you have come to the wrong spot. Here the gusts are strong. Even the curlew's cry is carried off."

"This is the right place to daze my wit."

"I must pile up this weed. That is no graceful endeavor."

"Elegance lies not in the task. It lies in how it is performed."

Brimhild flung back her head and laughed. It was a merry sound. "You are good, king. I can see all your years of diplomacy have sharpened your wordcraft."

"You are no innocent at speech skirmishes, although you are young."

"Your hall has whet my skills."

"Is it so treacherous?"

"For some," said Brimhild bitterly, thinking of Helga.

Hrothgar smiled. "Let me help you."

"You are the king!"

"I have undertaken much more physical work than you ever will. Seaweed and shit all have to be piled up and removed, or else they fill the house."

Brimhild smiled. "You are right about that, king."

"Don't call me that. I am Hrothgar. I am proud of my name and no one need be afraid to utter it." Brimhild nodded her assent. Hrothgar continued. "Perhaps you have labored in the kitchens long enough."

"I like it here by the sea."

"Why, mermaid?"

Brimhild did not look at him. Finally she said, "I lose myself in the wild waves. They draw me home."

"You are not kept here against your will, Brimhild."

"You know my name?"

"Yes. I saw you first when you had just come ashore. I thought you no antagonist then." He paused.

"And now?" She gazed at him directly.

"I hope you will be a sweet foe."

She laughed again. "I do not swallow such honeyed speech easily. I prefer the clean bitter tang of sea water. It is bracing and makes me alive."

"I will remember that, maiden."

As they spoke a dark body came closer. Brimhild saw it was Unferth. She shuddered and dared not look at him. He glowered at her. He knew his slave woman was linked to this girl. He was jealous of Helga's unforced affection for the maiden. "Hrothgar, it is time."

Hrothgar looked at Unferth and realized the hall needed his presence. "I must go," he apologized.

"I shall not stop you."

"I should like to stop your mouth with a kiss."

Brimhild could only roar with laughter. "You think I am a silly girl like those geese I must put up with in the kitchens? You may have conquered some of them with your cloying clauses. I was raised to admire the crabbed speech of the bard, the gnarled narrative of scaldic song. You are good, Hrothgar, at love language, yet you don't speak my tongue."

"Hrothgar," Unferth interrupted, "leave this wench. We must make plans. We sail tomorrow."

Brimhild swung her head around, fear in her eyes. Departure meant a trip in the longboats. That could only mean raiding parties and destruction.

"Yes, Brimhild," said Hrothgar, perceiving her gesture, "in the morning I must go. I don't know when I'll next be back. If ever."

"You never seem deficient in destruction, my lord."

"What do you mean by that?" asked Unferth angrily. "What does she mean by that?" he demanded of Hrothgar.

Hrothgar silenced him by raising his hand ever so slightly. "Go back to the hall. I will soon be there." His mouth was tight and grim.

Unferth was indignant at being sent off. He had to obey his master.

"What did you mean by that, Brimhild?" Hrothgar's voice was quiet and controlled. Brimhild felt a shiver.

"I mean, my lord, that when you return from such trips, women and children come with you. There are no husbands and fathers. Where are they? What happens to those you capture? Have you thought of them?"

"This is our way of life, Brimhild. It always has been and always will be. You cannot escape it."

"I can hate it, Hrothgar. And those who perpetuate it." She shot him a venomous glance.

Hrothgar only grinned. "I hope to change your mind when I return."

"If you do."

He started to go and then looked back at her. "It's true I may die. I would rather expire in your arms." He walked off into the night.

Brimhild could not help admiring him for his brazenness. "At least with such a man," she thought, "you know what he wants from you."

That night Hrothgar was distracted. The details of the raiding mission were bland and dull. Could it be Brimhild had stirred something in him besides desire? Is that why he could not sleep easily? Is that why plunder would lose its pleasure on this invasion?

Brimhild told no one, not even Helga, of what had passed

between them. She would not forget that ring-giver while he was absent.

Several weeks passed. When the party returned, there was a crush of activity in the kitchens: fowl and boar to be roasted, vegetables to cook, bread to bake. There was no shortage of amber liquor to wet the warrior's whiskered lips. Brimhild deliberately stayed in the outbuildings where the cooking preparations were underway. She took on any task. She did not want to see that chief of havoc.

At one point, when more loaves of bread were called for, a womb-heavy Helga drew Brimhild aside. She whispered, "Unferth is in no good temper."

"Why not? Wasn't the raid a success? Didn't they destroy and kill innocent people?"

"I don't know about that. So far I have seen no slaves. Unferth told me Hrothgar has gotten soft."

"What did he mean?" demanded Brimhild quickly.

"I don't know," answered Helga. "I only know Unferth is drinking even more than usual. He was in a fury. And Hrothgar can't keep still. He keeps looking around for something."

Brimhild's heart lurched. "Perhaps his newly fettered slaves," she said dryly, kneading bread and hoping desperately that Helga would not see her crimson cheeks.

"I must go," said Helga hurriedly. "Unferth may demand a visit tonight. If I can make him drunk, he will sleep." Off she went.

Odd, thought Brimhild, that Helga felt no resentment towards the child in her belly. That babe was an alloy of gold corselet and lead chains, wrought of lust and dread.

Brimhild could not help believing that Hrothgar was looking for her, seeking out the hostile maiden, fair flaxen beauty.

Later, there was a tumult in the kitchen. The girls were giggling and whispering hysterically. "He's coming," shouted one, wiping her floury hands on her apron. Another fixed her hair and smirked. The king was not unfamiliar with the beauties of the cookhouse.

"What is it?" Brimhild quietly asked Helga.

"Hrothgar is coming to the kitchens."

"Why?" she asked, knowing the answer.

"I think he wants to see how much food is left for the feasting," replied Helga, unsure that it was an accurate response.

Brimhild grabbed an extra apron to fling around her shoulders, and fled through the backdoor into the night. Lifting her skirts, she flew across the courtyard. The moon was large. The buildings gleamed. She could see her shadow. She escaped to the far distant shore, concealing herself between two dunes, the wrinkled sea mirroring the lunar lucence.

She was still breathing hard. Was she tempting him here? The other times they spoke were by the sea. Surely he would come. Surely he would find her. She hid where she knew he would find her. Yet she dreaded seeing him.

Then, some twenty feet off, she saw the tall figure, shattering her ken of the ocean. He was looking, seeking out her softness in the hummocks of sand. Then she heard him sing.

Cutting cold makes hard water,
sun melts frozen seas.
Flames char bones to dust,
fire roasts dripping meat.
Water drowns hapless sailors,
quenches thirsty men.
Earth splits apart,
cloven ground solid beneath our feet.
Winds extinguish heat's blaze,
freezing our limbs.
A sudden gust billows sails,
we race against the tide.

I listen, o fair one, to your moan,
now hear, I bid you, to mine.
Maid, let me love.
Maid, let me love.

Sigurd raised up that valiant woman,
encircled by flickering flames.
Like Brynhild I await your kiss
to wake into myself.
Maid, let me love.
Maid, let me love.

After the twilight of the gods,
all will be as new.
I've been destroyed,
consumed by wolf.
Come to me, my bitter love,
honey my lips with yours.
Found with me a guiltless throne,
a shining hall of mirth,
Maid, let you love.
Maid, let you love.

Hrothgar continued standing, looking out over the sea. He turned, contemplating the hollow between the sand mounds where Brimhild stood. They looked into each other's eyes. Only the breeze kept up a constant moan. Storm clouds covered the moon. All was suddenly dark. He was beside her, pressed up against her. When she felt his trembling, Brimhild stopped shaking.

Brimhild embraced him, held his head against her breast. He nuzzled her, she stroked him, kissing his hair. He lifted up his head. He gazed at her so that she quavered. Then, calm. The rain began softly. His lips brushed hers, her chest tightened, she could barely breathe. That delicious instant satiated her, infused with fear, pleasure, and desire.

She moved so quickly they were still kissing. She looked at him one last time, and ran off. She just ran and ran, the mist deepening to drizzle. She didn't stop until she collapsed, exhausted, gasping for breath, thoroughly soaked by rain, as awake as she had ever been in her life.

Taking shelter in a barn, she was found there the next morning by a farmer. Brimhild had fallen asleep in her wet clothes and woke up shivering, this time with fever. The farmer and his wife could make no sense of what she muttered in her illness and tended to her. For three weeks Brimhild ailed. Then she was conscious and realized she had wandered miles from that sand dune. She was still too weak to return. Another month passed before she could head off back to the hall.

And to her fate.

Just before she left, explaining that she was learning the life at court, the farmer and his wife told her of some visitors who had come while Brimhild was still out of her senses.

"There were two men, warriors they were. Unferth I knew by his bulk," said the farmer.

"What did they want?" asked Brimhild nervously.

"Apparently the king was frantically seeking out some woman. They winked and said it was no doubt a lusty wench, hence his urgency. You didn't look like a lusty wench to me."

"Certainly not in those sodden clothes and your hot brow," asserted his wife. "I popped right out and told them to get off our farm. We'd harbor no wanton women here."

Brimhild smiled. Hrothgar had sent out a search party. The lusty wench story was no doubt the invention of the dissolute Unferth. She walked slowly back to the hall in the sunshine over the course of the morning.

She crossed the fields to enter through the outbuildings, into the back kitchen door. All was busy. Flour spilled on the floor and girls were chattering and singing. Then, Helga saw her. "Brimhild!" she cried and ran up to greet her, embracing her. Her belly was round with child. Brimhild clutched happily to her friend. Then the others noticed Brimhild's arrival.

"She's back! We thought you'd run off with a pirate."

"Maybe I did."

"The king is furious with you."

"Furious?"

"Yes," said one of the girls, "as soon as you had disappeared he sent search parties out everywhere. What did you steal? Some furs or gold?"

"More likely his heart," muttered Helga into Brimhild's ear. Brimhild blushed.

"Just wait till he gets his hands on you!" said one of the others belligerently.

"I'm sure he'd like nothing better," whispered Helga and Brimhild pushed her away playfully, laughing.

"What makes you so wise?" asked Brimhild, once she and Helga had walked off alone together.

"Unferth told me. He said Hrothgar is almost crazy with grief—or desire." Brimhild felt strange, almost giddy.

Ealhhild came to her as soon as she had heard of Brimhild's return. "Well, what happened, my dear?"

Brimhild told her, leaving out the part about why she ran away, although Ealhhild had a fair notion of what had taken place. It made her respect the girl. "Why don't you sing tonight?"

"Sing, lady?"

"In the hall."

It was a peace offering from the queen mother. Here she was offering Brimhild a rare, privileged opportunity. She agreed to entertain. Ealhhild forbid the girls from telling of Brimhild's return. Her presentation was to be a surprise.

Chapter 7

The Riddle of Us

Ealhhild wove the peace that night, passing the mead-filled cup. Then she spoke. "Tonight the gods have smiled on us. The Æsir, Odin's kin, came of strange stock. Our singer, the shaper scop, will tell us of that first day, when the world was formed."

Ealhhild stepped aside. Behind stood Brimhild. She was dressed in dark blue robes, with gold torque encircling her throat, glittering clasp at her breast. Hrothgar stood in shock, frozen in disbelief and hope. Only the discipline of kingship prevented him from running to her. That training could not prevent tears from wetting his lids. If only her heavy clothes could soak up those briny beads as she sheltered him in her arms. Her red-gold hair glinted in the firelight. Hrothgar could have drunk that honey-mead gossamer.

Brimhild wove woman's words. She chanted of earth's creation, sea's source.

Heat met ice,
forming Ymir.
He lay asleep,
tired from his birth,
labor of discord.
He bore fruit,
a man and a woman under one arm,
a son with his leg.
From this frost ogre,
conceived by hostilities,
come all giants, evil ogres, grim and great.

From thawing frost emerged a cow.

Her teeming teats fed Ymir.
Cow tongue licked ice blocks,
savory with salt.
She melted free a man from the frozen blocks.
His grandson Odin
killed this Ymir,
whose hot blood, raging red, flaming force,
drowned all frost ogres,
save one.
Ymir's blood formed seas and lakes
his flesh the earth's foundation,
mountains arose from marrow mounds,
small stones from broken bones.
This is the story of middle-earth,
where men and women dwell.
We find our peace and home
in Ymir's cruel shell.
Remember this creation song,
this lady's loathsome lay,
that all of us depend for life
on bleeding, battered bones.

The men in the hall drank pensively. Only now did she dare look into Hrothgar's eyes. He had sunk back into his seat, staring at her, amazed at her safe return, an apparition from the dead. Brimhild sang of lovers' lore.

I look at the sea.
Your ship does not churn foam,
burst forth on the horizon.
You have gone to conquer lands.
Why did you not stay here
and master a softer foe?
Can you solve

the riddle of us,
this tangled enigma?

I chose you from all the men.
Music sways in your supple limbs.
Wind catches your long and curly hair.
You seem to have a love of song.
Can you solve
the riddle of us,
this tangled enigma?

The runic masters scratch their lines
onto sacred trees and rocks.
You've scraped into my white bones
your weird and magical lay.
Can you solve
the riddle of us,
this tangled enigma?

Yes, I can solve it, my beloved, answered Hrothgar's gaze to her questioning ballad.

The silence of the hall was shattered. "I would love to lay into your bones, lady!" shouted one sodden warrior.

Hrothgar immediately stood and touched his sword. At once the hall fell silent. The drunkard, Unferth, look shame-faced. He stood and bowed his head to Brimhild. "Forgive me, sweet singer. Your music transported me so that I thought I was the lucky fellow." Hrothgar still glowered at Unferth, who swayed tipsily. "But I'm just a drunken idiot." Everyone laughed, even Hrothgar and Brimhild.

"Will you sing to me always, Brimhild?" the king asked her that night, after he had caught up with her on the beach. She had been watching the dolphins leap in the moonlight, free in the watery playground.

"I don't know, my lord. One day I may return to my parents or marry and go away."

"Do you like to sing to me?" he asked.

"Yes, my lord. You seem to appreciate my verse."

"I don't want you to go away. I need your voice to awaken me."

"I am a free woman, my king."

"I am a captive. Be one with me. Be free no more. I beg you."

She considered for three days. Then she agreed to marry Hrothgar. Ealhhild was furious. Much as she admired the girl's integrity, she insisted that politics supercede the lure of love.

"Can't you see, my son," she asked, "how important it is to marry the daughter of a warring tribe? Only then can peace be woven."

"Brimhild comes from a foreign land."

"We have no idea which one."

"Mother, I don't have to live out your dead husband's life."

"He was your father!"

"I know. You were a peaceweaver and bore four children. And we have had little trouble with the Heathobards, haven't we?" he asked sarcastically.

"Not all such marriages work as planned. Think if I hadn't married your father! Then either my people or his would have been slaughtered, destroyed Danes or annihilated Heathobards. Surely small skirmishes are better than bloody butcherings."

Ealhhild remembered the first time she caught sight of Healfdene. The cruel king had killed her brother. She hated that husband, sheet sharer. Though Ealhhild had had no soft feelings for that husband, brother butcher, she consented to peaceweaving. To him she gave three boys and one girl. Only babies whose blood comes from enemy sides could build brotherhood, even when the bride was unhappy.

Hrothgar was determined. "She will be my bride, Mother.

Peaceweaving never works as it should. So why should I suffer? And she? Besides, I've conquered my enemies with no bride from the Heathobards or Franks or Swedes. My success can continue without some girl with guilty kin!"

The queen mother would not forget the worries that had plagued her at Brimhild's discovery. However, she admitted the old ways lived anew in Brimhild. The fair maid, bright as an elf, refused to be sullied by foreign fancies, though she herself was alien.

"Do you approve, Mother?" asked Hrothgar on the day of his marriage.

"Yes, son." Ealhhild hesitated. "She is beauteous. And retains the ancient magic."

"She bewitches me."

"Yet..."

"Yes, Mother?"

"I'd rather you'd have chosen an enemy's girl, foreign fancy. I fear for the future."

Hildilid and Sæwald had come to the court for several weeks before the wedding festivities. Aunt Ælfsciene came too.

"Do you love him, child?" asked Hildilid.

"Yes, Mother. He understands my soul. He weeps with me."

Auntie snorted. "A crying husband is no good!" She took Brimhild aside. "Do you know of love, child?"

"I have seen pigs and cows and horses, Auntie."

"Men are different. Don't be impatient for pleasure. It may never come. From your husband."

"Auntie! What do you mean?"

"I have had pleasure and I've never been wed."

"I love Hrothgar and mean to be a faithful wife. And loving."

"If you ever need my aid, Brimhild, come to me. I know potions which can make a man more virile." She whispered to Brimhild. "Take water agrimony and boil it in milk, that way you will excite his member. Or boil in ewe's milk water agrimony, alexanders, and the herb called Fornet's palm, then all will be as he most desires." Auntie giggled. "I also know potions to make him less virile, if that's what you'd prefer."

Hildilid gave Brimhild a wooden chest carved by Sæwald. Within were gowns, sumptuously embroidered by hand. Some had belonged to Hildilid years before at court. She had recut them to suggest the air of old fashion, freshened by sea-breezes. Buried among the gowns were several objects Brimhild had never seen before.

"What are these?" she asked.

"These were in the boat which saved you, my child."

"What are they?"

"That, as you can see, is a silver spoon. What it signifies, I don't know. The jewelry is remarkable though. The twisted gold has an exquisite design."

"And this book?"

"I cannot read. There, see, this mother and baby. I think it must be of you and your mother, my dear, before she had to give you up." Hildilid saw Brimhild's fascination with the illuminated picture. She felt a sudden loss. "Don't forget your father and me."

Brimhild snapped out of her reverie. "You will always be my mother. But she—" Brimhild could not finish. "What did she suffer?"

"Only love, my dear. All mothers do." Hildilid sang the last lullaby she would ever croon to her daughter before losing her to a man.

You washed up,
a piece of raw driftwood.
I've whittled you
with my love.
Here you belong.
Don't go back

to the icy waves.
They threw you away.
Remember?
You are my treasure,
once lost, now found,
I'll hold you by me
forever.

Brimhild stared at that picture long into the night by the glow of the seal oil lamp. Though she couldn't see herself in the baby's face, she could recognize a mother's love in the woman's gaze. "Why did you have to abandon me?" Brimhild asked the picture. "Where are you now?"

At the wedding, the shaman spoke of another marriage, unlike this one. "You all know how Thor's hammer was stolen by the giant Thrym. That large man refused to return the wonder weapon unless he got the lovely Freya for his bride. This angered the goddess of fertility. That lady's rage swelled her neck so much that her jewelled torque burst, scattering golden beads over the floor of Asgard, the gods' home. She refused to be wed against her will.

"Loki suggested that Thor dress as the beauteous maid, though he resisted concealing his manly strength. The hammer was necessary for the gods' survival. He dressed as Freya. The welcoming banquet was a feast. Thor consumed an ox and eight pink salmon. The giant was confounded by his bride's appetite. 'Oh,' proclaimed Loki, 'the little lady was so thrilled to marry you, she has fasted for a week and a day. Her real hunger is for you.' The giant grinned with pleasure.

"He approached his intended, lifting her veil to plant his giant lips on her girlish ones. He was dismayed to see Thor's fearsome flaming eyes stare out at him. 'Oh,' hastened Loki to explain, 'Freya is so eager to hold you against her lissom body that she has not been able to sleep for a week and a night.' This pleased the lascivious giant to start the festivities.

"A bridal couple is hallowed by a hammer laid in the bride's lap. When this secret bride had his hammer again, he stood up. The flowing gown molted from his godly frame. Soon the giant's party lay in ruins, massive bodies piled dead on the floor. Thor wore bridal linen, then slew the sister of giants. She got no golden rings, only the shock of hammer. Thor returned triumphant to Asgard. Loki's trick had succeeded.

"Today's marriage is a union of two bodies and their kin. Hrothgar is our king, fearless in battle. Now the Scyldings rule distant lands that pay tribute to our glory. Brimhild returns to us the traditional ways. Graceful custom is no stranger to her."

Brimhild was hallowed by Thor's hammer. Though laid in her lap, she did not wield the hammer as did the disguised god to attack the giants.

The chief Priest spoke: "High Thunderer, consecrate this marriage through your might. The sign of the hammer you make over the bones and skin of your goats after feasting to restore them to life. Bring new life to this man and woman through your divine intervention."

After the ceremony, the queen mother, Ealhhild, held the ceremonial cup. Bearing it aloft, she presented golden mead to Hrothgar, his bride, her parents, then Unferth and Æschere the counsellors. She returned to Brimhild. "Now you, newly minted queen, weave a web of peace for your marriage bed and lord's land." Brimhild had been well-trained by her mother. She had long practiced with her dolls, little knowing that one day she would commit the ceremony as a true act, no pretend play. Never again would Ealhhild present the honeyed cup. That was now Brimhild's brew.

The scop sang. Signy and Hagbard, loving friends, were divided by her father. They longed without hope. Against all reason they were betrothed. A secret against the father can only bode ill. Hagbard was seized, the daughter's cries were in vain.

Condemned to his doom, he proclaimed his link to Signy, forged in their hearts. "I'll die, too," she cried, "and lie with you in death." She fashioned her fate. Before he was hanged, Hagbard asked for a favor. "Allow me to see," he pled, "if Welend's smithy lives up to its fame." He wanted to know if the bonds binding them would break like his breath. The fated man saw the flames of the woman's home. She burned herself to ashes as he rode the gallows. That artisan, the linker of lovers, had done good work.

The scop sang a new song. "Of Modthryth I'll sing."

"Oh, yes, that wench with her foolish ways," roared a drunken Unferth.

"Men came to her, to seek her fair hand. Never a one would she choose. Each would visit Valhalla's halls after failing to conquer her charms. At last the arch-Angle, Offa, made her his wife. He conquered that peerless princess in bed-battle. She abandoned her strife."

"As if an Angle king could conquer a woman!" The hall broke into laughter at the thought of that.

Ealhhild, the queen mother, stood. "I know a loose lay to brighten the hall." She clapped her hands to a bawdy ballad.

In ancient days when Romans ruled,
women had no say.
Their song was sung
in dumbshow,
their listeners blind and deaf.
Now we call upon our men
to hold us hot and hard,
demand our nightly naughtiness.

"We'll obey you, lady," shouted out one besotted battler.

We take back the bridal bed.
Don't think the blushing virgin

hates her husband's heat,
for women savor their moments
rooted in desire.
If you come to us
with laughing eyes and eager loins
don't leave us languishing anight
to pillage and rape.
Else your child may have
the cobbler's eye
or the tailor's chin.

With this merriment as a melody for the start of their marriage, the couple left their retainers and friends.

In their bedchamber, Hrothgar presented Brimhild with his golden ring. "This is the ring of my youth for you to carry. It is pressed with an image of the hammer of Thor." Brimhild took it and had it strung on a golden chain, an amulet she always wore around her neck, next to her heart.

Her most precious pearl he plundered that eve. A more willing victim would be hard to imagine.

The web was spun. A period of peace ensued.

This once happened; so, too, this will pass.

II. The Hall-Queen

I suffer crime, I enjoy mother's flesh....I seek my father, my mother's husband, my wife's daughter, and do not find them.

Riddle from the Old English *Apollonius of Tyre*

My daughter will one day marry. I hope she marries no king or lord. I'd rather she marry a man like Sæwald or my husband, men who fish in boats. Salt-water is fresh, the sea-breeze clean. There is no savage smoke like that from the meadhall fire. The court is an enclave from the icy bleakness of winter. Yet it houses a chill which bites more sharply than the sunless winds—of indolent warriors, threatened prayer men, and rival women. Stay by the sea, my child, shun the gilded hall! A hut with a peat fire, fish stew, and the honey mead of peace and sufficiency fulfills the soul better than the nervous maneuverings for power within the sphere of the ring-giver. The hall may offer the glory of singing scops and solemn ceremony. The humble hut cradles you in a simple life, warm bed, and eager husband.

Hear, my daughter, of the fate of Brimhild. She had her glory and her fame, then her ruin and her shame.

Chapter 8

Spinning Fate

The year had its own rhythm. To maintain peace one has to conquer. The spring planting, then Hrothgar's summer trip of plundering and raiding. Back home for the autumn harvest, then the early winter pillage and ransack. In this way, over the half-years, Hrothgar had built up a large kingdom, one that rivaled that of his great-grandfather, Scyld Scefing, a pirate of extraordinary rapacity and talent, ravenous wolf.

Brimhild did not ask what happened on these trips. She preferred not to know. She surely knew of the twisted gold and coiled jewelry he returned with, the boats of alien design, the clothes of foreign cut. One misty morning upon her husband's return, she saw a mass of women and children, dark and hopeless, marched past the women's quarters.

She went to speak to Hrothgar. "I've come, my lord, to speak to you."

"Brimhild!" he exclaimed, grabbing her around the waist and stroking her breast. She pushed him away. "You are formal."

"It is a matter of form which compels me to speak with you."

Hrothgar sensed her seriousness. "What is it, my love?"

Brimhild hardly knew how to begin. Make it simple, she thought. "It is this new batch of slaves, Hrothgar."

"What about them? Is there one you want?"

"No! Surely you know I am against the killing and trading of human flesh! I freed Helga. I wish to free these poor creatures as well."

"What? They do not belong to me alone. They belong to my men."

69

"Then buy them from your retainers. Let me do so."

"Brimhild," he said, as though speaking to a child, "you don't understand how these things work."

"I understand all too well. I have not asked what you do on these trips, though I can imagine. I want the killing and humiliation to end."

"If they end, our kingdom ends."

"Then so be it."

Now Hrothgar was in a fury. "You are so moral. We brutal men keep you safe and secure and fed. Those slaves belong to the Heathobards who, only last winter killed the men of a Scylding fishing village and stole their wives and children. Are we to just sit here and allow such actions go unpunished?"

"You can turn your cheek aside."

"What? What nonsense are you speaking?"

"A priest once told me that."

"A priest? What priest?"

"Not of our faith," she admitted.

"Then why even say it? You know our system. If someone transgresses, they must pay wergild or expect us to avenge the action. That is life, dear. And I thought you were all for the old ways. This is as old as it gets."

"It could be different."

"How?" Hrothgar was skeptical.

"We could send some counsellors there to negotiate a peace settlement."

Hrothgar laughed. "We have a peace settlement, Brimhild. This is as peaceful as it gets. At least we are the winners. You would be singing a different tune if we were the losers. Then you would be all for bloodshed."

Brimhild shook her head. "I wouldn't. No matter who they killed."

"Really?" Hrothgar gazed at her through hooded eyes. "I wonder. I think everyone has a point where they could kill or avenge. Even you, my sweet," he said gently, standing and holding her close.

She was stiff and unresponsive. "I want to buy their freedom," she said in a very low voice.

"I forbid it," said Hrothgar, murmuring into her hair. "I am your lord and the leader of the Scyldings." He kissed her ear and she pulled away. "Brimhild!" She walked off. "Brimhild!"

A month later Unferth showed up with gold and furs, enough to make even the meanest farmer of Hrothgar's realm a warm and cossetted man. The children had disappeared. Only one slave woman remained with him. She was his new pleasure.

By this time Helga had borne her rich fruit — a son named Skjold after the legendary king. "Conceived in servitude, he may live to rule his father," said Helga as she nursed him.

Unferth came to retrieve the child. Brimhild met him at the door. "What do you wish?"

"That is my son. I will raise him. I am the father. He was conceived when Helga was still enslaved. That makes him a slave, despite her status now."

Unferth's gross bluster could not frighten the queen. "His mother is a free woman, released by me. The child was likewise freed by me upon his birth. You cannot enslave those set free by others," pointed out Brimhild. "Besides, the child needs the mother's milk."

"I have a new concubine. She can nurse him. She just lost a child," explained Unferth.

"No doubt at your will. You cannot take with one hand and give with the other." Brimhild had no fondness for him.

Unferth glowered at Brimhild. "You are only the queen. The king will decide." The burly man stomped off. The baby cried at Helga's terror.

Brimhild consoled her, "That man will not possess your child."

Later, Hrothgar held counsel. He heard from Unferth and from Brimhild, standing in for the mother who watched nervously as she suckled the newborn. The king was silent for many minutes. Then he spoke. "It is foolish to bicker over a newborn's life in such a fashion. He may easily die, as so many infants do, from disease or war. To decide his fate, we must use common sense. Helga and Unferth both are free. The child was born a slave, yet released into freedom. Thus, we must determine his fate as best suits him, not the parents. A young child, girl or boy, needs the mother for nurturing at least. I have considered when a boy needs his father. The concept of fostering is not foreign to us. When a lad reaches the age of ten or twelve, he is sometimes sent here, to the court, to learn of ways of warriors and kings. Then he is no longer with his mother. His father may visit periodically, but usually the child accompanies another older man who teaches him the ways of the soldier and counsellor.

"Skjold will need a father once he is ten or so. Until that time, his mother may keep him. Then, the child may be trained by his father. My hope is that this formal ruling need not prevent a fluid exchange between the child and both parents. After all, both Helga and Unferth live in the hall. The child will, as a matter of course, see both mother and father frequently. It is best for a son to accept both sides of his engendering, not to make war between distaff and spear. I charge you, Helga and Unferth, not to meddle in your son's affections for the other parent, or else I will take the son into my own keeping. And Unferth," added Hrothgar with a malicious smile, "you need not be so greedy for that son of yours. After all, you have a luscious concubine to warm your bed." That woman did not smile, though the men in the hall guffawed.

Displeased with Hrothgar's decision, Unferth had to abide by it. Helga was delighted that she need not worry about losing her child for many years. Brimhild was grateful to Hrothgar. He protested that he would have acted in this way despite her influence. "A child needs both parents. Unferth, though a cunning counselor, is no tender man for a baby begot by force." The queen wondered how the king knew of Skjold's begetting.

Brimhild was always busy. When Hrothgar was gone, she ruled in his stead, guided by counselors too old to seize spoils, pluck prize. She watched over the running of the household. Baking, brewing, spinning, and weaving were all done within the confines of her estate. No longer was she a hall girl. She was the queen, court consort, royal ruler. She remembered how low she had felt, apprenticed to Hrothgar's hearth. To make the learning process better for the girls, she limited the hours they had to perform physical labor, made sure an older woman mentored a younger in courtly ways, and visited with each one weekly to hear her concerns, worries, and complaints. She wanted her girls to be shining Scyldings, lovely ladies, famous females. Hrothgar's glory would gleam all the brighter reflected in their glow.

Ealhhild, her mother-in-law, did not interfere with Brimhild's projects. "I will die soon, Brimhild. You need to prepare for that day. Ask me for help now, while I still can speak and remember the past."

"What would you tell me, lady?"

"I did not love Hrothgar's father. Loving a king can interfere with your obligations. Nothing troubled my trust. Duty was my only guide. I was never distracted by lust or desire. Only my children counted. I was a good queen! You love my son. I pity you, my dear. I believe that affection will destroy you both one day. It is best for rulers to marry for peace. The only true marriage is between a ruler and his land."

Brimhild was amused by the old lady's thoughts. She knew that love lay at the heart of any successful kingdom. The young queen controlled her comments carefully. "Thank you, lady, for your concern. Peace is my utmost concern. I wish Hrothgar's realm to be a fecund field, his reign to be properous, his memory that of a chosen chief."

"Still," muttered Ealhhild, "I wish you were a foe's female. So does peace prosper, so is favor fertilized." Ealhhild spoke, looking into the past. "A woman may see the man and feel her desire. Her thighs may quiver as she presses him close. Such is not the way to marry. Such is not the way to wed.

"Love whom you choose. But pick as your groom only the enemy, only the adversary, only the treaty breaker, only the antagonist. For that marriage alone can weave a peace, that bride alone can help her land, that man alone can heal ancient wounds.

"You love your husband, you yearn for my son. That union is selfish. It undoes my wedding winters ago. It lays waste to my children born of that match. I disdained my husband. For that, our rule was no failure.

"A woman who favors her man hates her country. The queen who lusts for the king betrays her people. She'll mind if he fights, since he may die. She'll worry if he journeys, since he may drown. She'll fret if he treaties, since he may forget her.

"Learn to be indifferent, my dear, or your fate is ill-spun."

Brimhild made efforts to spin a good fate for her land and her marriage. To help her people, Brimhild summoned Ælfsciene to the hall. "Help me, Auntie. We need to cure the people of the land who are sick. I am asking if you would travel over foamy waves, test tides. Visit our people and make the sick well, the dying comfortable. I will let our people know they can come to this hall for relief. You taught me medical means, helpful herbs, when I was a girl. I will heal the land, slay sickness."

Ælfsciene agreed, adding, "Remember, a fatal sickness no doctor can cure, no matter how many herbs she has. A charm will favor no patient, if he is doomed, fated by fortune."

The people flocked to the hall, seeking out Brimhild's medical magic. She helped her people, succored Scyldings. When Ealhhild died, withered by age, fatigued by frailty, Brimhild eased her passing.

Brimhild, however, could not heal herself. She still had not yet born fruit. Hrothgar, Scylding's protector, was displeased. "In olden times, the hero Rerir begot heroes. He was the grandson of Odin. Rerir's wife also could not become fecund. Then a wish-maiden dropped an apple into Rerir's lap. That helped his wife conceive. We need a wish-maiden to grant us our desire." Later Rerir's son, Volsung, married that wish-maiden, his wife-mother.

Hrothgar suggested that they pray to the gods. She agreed that they must plead with Frija, wife of Odin, goddess of fertility. She failed in her job as a queen without bearing an heir for the peace of the Honor-Scyldings. Frija, who brought peace and fertility to the land, would be their guide.

They tried different charms and recipes to help Brimhild conceive. She drank wine with the dust of a female hare's belly weighing as much as four pennies, while Hrothgar drank a similar potion with the dust of a male hare's belly. They had intercourse with one another and then abstained. Brimhild took a parsnip and boiled it in water, which they then bathed themselves in.

Not conceiving, Brimhild went to the barrow of a deceased man, stepped thrice over it, then said three times:

Let this heal me
of hideous slow labor.
Let this heal me
of grueling painful labor.
Let this heal me
of bitter unfinished labor.

Then Hrothgar bound the lower part of henbane on her left thigh, near her vulva, along with twelve grains of coriander seed.

When these remedies failed, Hrothgar turned to an older magic, a stronger and more potent one. "In days of yore, the goddess Nerthus reigned here in Denmark supreme. This was before the Romans held sway, or the Vandals wrecked havoc on our shores. I have heard of a secret cult, which worships her still. Let it shower us with ancient truths, so your belly can grow big."

Brimhild trusted her royal consort. He would know of such a group, of course, with his spies and contacts throughout the land.

A strange and frightening priest appeared. "Nerthus resides in her chariot, a wagon we strew with flowers and vines. Around the land of the Spear-Danes we will travel. Only I may see inside the wagon, for I alone know when the goddess is present, shielded from earthly glare within. She brings fertility to all. She will bring a flowering to your land. I will need some slaves to assist me. They will feed the oxen that pulls her wagon. They will gather food for me and the goddess, provide shelter, care for the animals. Never will they see the Earth Goddess, Mother of Magic."

Brimhild readily agreed and sent him her favorite servants, all former slaves. "For such an important journey and sacred trek as this," she told them, "I need only my most trustworthy friends." They happily assented to assist in this fertilizing of the land. Helga volunteered to go along as well.

And so throughout Hrothgar's realm the sacred chariot made its rounds. Laborers paused in their fields, sailors came ashore, to rejoice at the presence of Nerthus, long-forgotten queen of abundance. Everywhere she went, revelry ensued. In remote spots, orgies were rumored. It is true that one year later, more children were born to the Bright-Danes than was usual.

At last the chariot pulled up outside the hall itself. Hrothgar and Brimhild prayed with the priest's blessing for a fertile bed. The priest stood before the gathering and chanted:

"O Divine goddess, Nature's nurturer, who makes the sun and moon glisten in the sky above us here below, you bring all things forth. Make the Scylding land fecund and fruitful, foster fertility and let seeds find rich soil. You control the chaos of the elements, you train the wind and the rain and the shadows, you bring light and shame the night. When our souls depart from earth, we return to your nurturing bosom. You are the mother of the gods, we adore you."

After this blessing, all present in the hall drank and made merry. Many were the rumpled sheets in the morn.

The next day the goddess was to return to her sanctuary. The priest chose a lake, a short journey from the hall. In the center of this shimmering pool was a small island, Walcheren, green grove to the gods. Brimhild and Hrothgar came to watch the ritual washing. Ælfsciene joined them, gazed at the goddess's wagon. "I have only heard tell of these ancient rites, worship of old. Now I see the cleansing of sacred shores."

The servants washed the priest's vestments, the chariot, and themselves. "Now," proclaimed the priest, so all could hear, "the goddess herself must be cleansed."

"I thought they couldn't see the goddess," exclaimed Brimhild quietly to Ælfsciene.

"They may but for an instant," answered Ælfsciene cryptically.

The former slaves, far from shore now, looked into the chariot. The shore travellers saw their looks of astonishment even across the liquid ripples. They carried water into the divine dray, sluicing the floor of the goddess's carriage. When they had finished, the priest uttered words, held up his hands and beckoned them into the icy loch. Out to their waists the servants surged forward, four in all, male and female. Then when the chanting and prayers had ended, the priest embraced the first one by his side. The priest leaned him back and held his face beneath the waves. Though the servant struggled, the priest was no weak retainer of the gods. Bubbles frothed the lake's surface. Finally, there were none. The body floated. The priest made his next lethal embrace.

Brimhild could not understand at first. Then the shock passed away. "Hrothgar! He's killing them!"

"This is our Mother Earth's demand for our defiance of her. A purifying of our sins."

"They have done nothing wrong. Do something!" She turned to her aunt. "Ælfsciene! Surely you agree."

Ælfsciene only stared at the drownings. "This is the old way, the ancient lost way. In it is sadness with hope."

Brimhild started for the pond, to rescue Helga at least. Hrothgar held her, grappled with his beloved. At last the sacrifice was perfect, complete. The earth goddess had taken her exaction.

Brimhild stood frozen, still embraced by Hrothgar's fleshly fetters, horrified by the barbarity. "How could he?" she finally managed to utter. She looked at Hrothgar. "How could you?" Hrothgar let her go. She ran to Helga and the others, all lost. No medicine could save them now. She removed Helga's necklace. Later she added the amber bead to her own necklace. It nestled against her breast, by the ring of Thor. "I won't ever forget you, Helga," she vowed.

She remembered Ealhhild's words. If only she hadn't loved her husband, this betrayal would mean nothing to her. Because she cared, she ached.

As time passed, Brimhild grew pregnant. Perhaps the goddess had aided the prosperity of that pregnancy. Hildilid and Ælfsciene came to help with the delivery, arriving as soon as Brimhild knew of her condition. Auntie helped Brimhild prepare for a healthy birth. "Now you must go to your lord in bed and say,

Above I step,
straddling you I go,
with living child,
not with a dying one,
with one in full bloom,
not with a doomed one.

"This will help the child to be healthy."

While Brimhild did as was bidden her, trusting Ælfsciene's medical skill, she could not forget her aunt's passivity in the face of those killed. Perhaps, thought Brimhild, one who had witnessed so much suffering, so much death, no longer saw the dying as people needing aid. Perhaps Ælfsciene forgot the specific soul, the single sufferer, thinking the sacrifice would help the common good. Brimhild hoped she would never reach that point herself.

Ælfsciene was concerned with what Brimhild ate. "Eat nothing salty or sweet. Don't drink beer and certainly don't get drunk! Don't consume swine's flesh. Don't eat any fat. Don't ride too much on a horse or the child will come too early.

"Don't eat nuts or acorns or any fresh fruit in the fifth month or the child will be an idiot," she warned. Other advice she added as well. "If you eat bull or ram's meat, that of the buck or boar, or cock's or gander's flesh, then it sometimes happens that the child is humpbacked!" Auntie also tried to determine the sex of the fetus. "You are carrying a boy if you walk slowly and have hollow eyes. If you go quickly and have swollen eyes, it's a girl." Then Brimhild's aunt got a lily and a rose and held them out to her. "Choose one of these flowers."

"Why, Auntie?"

"Just do so."

Though Brimhild thought it was foolish, she chose the rose. "Ah ha, it's a girl!" shouted Ælfsciene.

"Why?" asked Brimhild.

"Because you chose the rose! If you had chosen the lily, we would know it's a boy." Ælfsciene also observed how Brimhild walked. If she stepped more with her heels on the ground, it would be a boy; if with her toes, a girl. If the belly is high up, it's a boy; if sunk down, a girl.

Ælfsciene told Brimhild how in the first six weeks, the brain of the fetus grows in the womb, then a membrane covers it. In the second month, the veins are formed, three hundred and sixty-five of them. In the third month, the fetus is a man without a soul. In the fourth month, he is firm in his limbs. Ælfsciene warned Brimhild how in the fifth month, the fetus grows quickly, making the mother witless. In the sixth month he gets a skin, and the bones grow. His toes and fingers develop in the seventh month. Then the breast organ grows and his heart and blood.

When time came for the delivery, her mother and Auntie had prepared many potions. Some were to help remove the placenta after delivery. Others were to hasten the birth along, since, if the child does not come out, it turns in the belly to a deadly disorder, most often on a Tuesday evening.

They prepared three places at the table. "Who is coming?" asked Brimhild in her pain.

"The Norns," answered Ælfsciene. "Fate, Being, and Necessity. They live beneath the World Tree whose fruits are burned and help women in labor. I have brought you a brew with a pinch of this fruit. It is very precious and will help you in your agony."

Brimhild sipped the potion. Ælfsciene chanted, "May what is within pass out!"

The pain was hard and long. So is winter. Spring inevitably arrives no matter how thick the frost. Women helped the womb-bound lady, strong spells they spoke. Hildilid and Ælfsciene dissolved dried hare's heart into warm water and fed it to Brimhild, so that her pain would ease. They seethed old lard in water and bathed her vulva with it. Then she drank hollyhock boiled in ale. These potions eased her pains after birth. In such a way did Oddrún, Atli's sister, aid Borgny. That mother's twins could not pass out until the midwife, grieving for Gunnar, sang splendid spells.

Brimhild bore a son, which pleased Hrothgar. "Though a girl would be just as welcome, my bride. A warrior-boy or peaceweaving girl—both bless a conquering kingdom."

Ælfsciene wondered at his sex. "But Brimhild had chosen the rose!" Yet the son grew well and tall. He had flaxen hair from Brimhild's foreign stock. He was a loving, sweet child. As he grew it became clear: he was a beautiful boy. His loveliness caused girls to envy him. Long, thin, pale fingers, finely muscled torso, he was a beauteous youth. He brought unmitigated joy to both Brimhild and Hrothgar who trained him in the manly arts.

Brimhild also taught him the womanly arts. "If you can sing and tell a tale well, my son, it could save your life one day. Your father fell in love with me because I sang of sadness long since which pierces me yet. Perhaps the girl you love will find you the same way."

The Norns fixed his fate, spun his fate-thread, allotted his life. Ravens, wolves, and eagles rejoiced at his birth. This was a hero indeed!

Chapter 9

All Creation Wept

Meanwhile, Unferth's brother Coifi returned after an absence of more than twenty half-years. He had been kidnapped by Irish pirates when Brimhild was a girl. He arrived with a new name: Jerome. "What a funny name," complained Unferth, Ecglaf's son. "Why do you shed your true name for a false one?"

"Because now I know my true self. I am a follower of Christ the Messiah." He told what had happened in his absence. Once in Ireland, after his shaman status was made clear, he was sent to live with priests on a wild, rocky outcropping. There he heard the Bible. At first he could not understand the Irish. The priests used a second language more important than their mother tongue: Latin. So Jerome had to master both languages, which he readily did by working menial tasks in the priests' havens. One day he spontaneously uttered a song in Latin about the Christ. He was soon made a priest in the Roman faith.

Jerome told of Baldr, the most beloved of his own people's gods, the beauteous fated boy. All the gods loved Baldr. At his birth, all living creatures promised not to harm him. Sadly, his mother had forgotten to ask the plant mistletoe to withhold its dread doom. One day, when Baldr was sixteen, the gods played one of their favorite games. As Baldr was, they thought, invulnerable, they would shoot arrows at him as he dashed laughing through the hall. Loki, god of trickery, gave the blind god an arrow made of mistletoe. When it was shot, the pin pierced Baldr and poisoned his fair limbs. He died. He would be revived only if all creation wept. And so, too, the Christ died with all the world in mourning. Yet he arose again to reign and save.

Jerome told this story, as well as others, to the court. He told how his Christian way was the true one. If Hrothgar wanted to enter the world as a progressive ruler of the best folk, he needed to convert and not remain the leader of a superstitious backwater.

This kind of talk angered the hall's shaman. Yet Jerome could not be entirely ignored, as he had once been head shaman. The queen mother, Ealhhild, had died. Everyone knew she would have rejected this Christianity as a weird and dangerous belief. Hrothgar adhered to the old way.

"Jerome has good ideas," said Brimhild.

"You say that? I thought you always maintained that the old ways were best." Hrothgar was incredulous, reluctant to disrupt his realm with a new belief system.

"I know, Hrothgar. The customs of yore are good and beautiful." Yet she had not forgotten the fertility rites, deadly destruction. "A new way is coming. I sense it."

Furthermore, though she did not tell Hrothgar, there were those strange artifacts in her mother's chest, left to Brimhild by her first family. Some of them started to make sense. Jerome's teachings had made clear that the symbolism of the two lines, one horizontal and one vertical, at right angles to each other, symbolized the cross on which the Christ died. Why it was on a spoon, she didn't know.

The new way caused some adherents to the gods of Odin to grumble. Jerome destroyed the idols in their temples, though not the sacred buildings themselves. The pagan places he purified, sprinkled them with holy water. Altars he set up in them, crafted crucifix, wrought rood. Once, as they sat in the hall, bitter words were spoken about these matters.

Jerome explained. "Rome wants us to encourage heathen hope. By keeping their shrines, shriven by Christ, they may come to see the True Way. All we lack are relics, saints' bones, proof of God's goodness."

"I can provide bones for your God, Jerome, just name the day," threatened Unferth, furious disciple of Freyr.

Jerome laughed, believing blood could not be spilled between brothers. Yet Cain killed Abel in his Bible, sacred source. Unferth accused Jerome of treachery. This coming from a man most like Loki, the god who caused Baldr's death, prevented his rebirth.

Loki had given birth to three monsters. His first child was Fenrir, the wolf. That was no good dog. He will one day consume Odin. Another child was the Midgard Serpent. He will break loose at the end of the world. Hel was Loki's daughter. She rules Niflheim. The old and diseased journey there once they breathe no more.

Like Loki, Unferth would birth monstrous acts, fraternal betrayal.

"Yet, brother," countered Jerome, "is it treachery to wish my earthly lord to live eternally with our heavenly Lord?" Unferth's scowl darkened. "After all, the old gods have not always kept faith with us. I can remember many times praying and making obeisance to them, with nary a result."

Brimhild wanted to know more of this religion. Hrothgar did not want her to indulge this strange way.

Suddenly a sparrow flew into the hall, dipped down through the light near the fire's warmth, and out again into the winter storm.

Æschere, Hrothgar's rune counselor, closest companion, spoke. "Like that sparrow, we too enter this warm and welcoming world from a cold and mysterious origin. And after our death, like the sparrow fleeing our presence, a wintry night, an undiscovered country, awaits us all. Is it not best to pray for a life which is light and filled with warmth beyond this short transient pain?"

Ælfsciene proclaimed, for all to hear, "Thor has delivered a challenge to your Jesus to meet him in single combat. That is how warriors come to determine the truth for a nation's future."

Jerome replied, "My lord has already fought, and he lives again. Can your god do that?"

Hrothgar agreed that more of this religion should be explored. He allowed Brimhild to take lessons with Jerome. He ordered Æschere, his most trusted counselor, to attend them and report back.

So Jerome told of his Lord's story. Brimhild tried to adapt the Christian story to her pagan gods. Æschere teased her cumbersome efforts. Jerome taught them about the Greek and Roman gods, along with Latin, so they could hear of the Lord's will, as so many true believers did. He instructed them to write the Roman letters in the sand, for there it was easy to correct their errors. The beach they inscribed was erased twice daily by the incoming tide, so no one would know of their secret written language.

As time went on, Unferth's antagonism swayed Hrothgar. Brother threatened brother. "Perhaps it is the expedient thing to leave for a while," counseled Æschere to Jerome, "until your brother calms down."

That night, Jerome was called to Brimhild's chamber. "Can you keep a secret?" she asked the priest.

"Yes, lady. I speak only to God of private words."

"Then let me show you these." Brimhild opened her wooden chest. On top of the delicate woolens lay her mystery treasures. "Tell me, priest, if you can, what these are."

Jerome held up the glittering silver object and the book. He explained it seemed to be a christening spoon, used to baptize new Christians.

"And the book?"

He read aloud in a chanting, mesmerizing tongue. "It is Latin, lady. The Gospel of Luke."

"Who is this lady in the picture? And the baby?"

Brimhild was disappointed to learn it could not be her own mother, but the Virgin Mary. Yet she was heartened to think some question of her birth might be solved. She told Jerome of her coming to Hrothgar's realm. He remembered it well.

"Then, lady, you must have had Christian parents."

"Yes, yes, it is clear."

"And you, lady, might be Christian yourself. Perhaps you were baptized with this very spoon."

It was clearly so, yet Brimhild was shocked to hear it spoken aloud. Naturally she was brought into the new way by her folk, else they would not have left such valuable goods with her.

"How can I know who my folk are?"

"Lady, I have seen such silverwork before. It is of the Jutish folk. I am to leave here soon. I feel the court's hostility to my words. Perhaps if I make a migration, much as the Irish priests do, I can learn more about God. I may go to the realm of the Jutes. I will ask if they know of a mermaid such as you. Not many women could have sent their babes afloat. Do not despair—I will try to find your people. They are Christians and alien to these lands—yet you want to know of your father and mother. Perhaps you have siblings, lady. I will find out if I can."

"Thank you, Jerome. How can I repay you?"

Jerome thought a moment. "The new way is strange to barbaric superstition. I once thought our gods supreme. Then, Jesus's love touched me. Few men raised by Odin's mark can sense the gentle Christ's symbol. Ladies are drawn to him. Most kings listen to their Christian brides and agree to the new way. Present the lore to Hrothgar."

"I know so little. And the old way is still mine own."

"Be open to God's love, lady. That is all I ask."

Jerome melted into the night. The next day Unferth angrily demanded all at court to tell where his brother went. "I must save my foolish brother from his wayward thoughts. Ragnarök, the end of the world, will come to consume him for his foolishness."

Brimhild spoke. "Dear friend of Hrothgar, Jerome spoke to me. Often, he says, the Irish priests of his faith make a wandering to seek out God's truth. He has revealed to me his intention to do so. I do not know when he plans to return, or if he even will do so. Perhaps the raven will pick at his bones on some alien shore."

"Can I hear these words and not be angered?" shouted Unferth.

"Now, my queen," said Hrothgar sternly, "such thoughts do not console Unferth in his grief."

"He does not seem to grieve for his kin whose every hope for the court's conversion was treated as poison," replied Brimhild.

"Do you think this teaching is worthy of us?" demanded Unferth.

"The question may be," said Brimhild quietly, "are we worthy of it?"

After these words were spoken, Unferth had no soft regard for the queen.

Chapter 10

Glittering Gables

During this time, Brimhild suggested to Hrothgar that he celebrate the success of his reign with a glorious structure—a meadhall for joyous ceremonies. It would help unite all the retainers, including those opposed to the new way. She confessed in her heart the desire to establish her stability as a queen of the traditions of the past, especially since some questioned her devotion to the old ways, holy habits. Her interest in a new religion nipped at the old, just as Fenrir gobbled Tyr's hand.

The hall should gleam with gold.

We have learned of such shining gold, miraculous metal Loki paid as ransom for the dead otter. Only gold would suffice as wergild. The grieving father demanded the miraculous metal for his son's slaughter. Loki sought out the elf, destructive dwarf. He cursed that gold ring, sinister circle, doom deliverer. Later one brother would spur Sigurd, make murder, fashion fratricide. That would not be the last kin killing, begotten by gold. The glittering yellow metal dazzles the senses, makes mayhem, works revenge.

The foundation of the hall was laid not far from the old main hall which they would use until the new one was built. It sat higher on the headland, so that longships could gaze at it awestruck in terror and wonderment from the sea. Artisans both local and from across the water would be hired to complete this masterpiece. Brimhild thrilled to see them at work—measuring, carving, painting. She took her son with her to watch and supervise the work. Though only a child, he loved the beauty of the wood and the tune of the tool.

The new hall was to be twice the size of the old, reflecting the growth of Hrothgar's kingdom—regal retainers and loyal ladies flocked to his walls in this time of prosperity and peace. Older shabby buildings were torn down and sturdier outbuildings were constructed. A new kitchen was the heart of the outbuildings with burnt-clay ovens. They were dome-shaped, like beehives forged with mead-rich honey. The old hall would be taken over by the women for their sleeping quarters.

Brimhild believed this hall would stand as a symbol for her husband's kingdom, a glorious glittering grail, achievement of peace and grace. She hoped the hall would anchor Hrothgar, so that he would diminish or even halt the spring and autumn raiding trips. The thriving, humming nature of the hall project invigorated and excited Brimhild.

She met scops who wandered through, having heard tell of the magnificent hall which, when finished, would need the poet's harp to resound. They would visit, staying several nights, weeks, or months. Brimhild duly noted their names and whence they originated. The building would take time, and fine musicians must be gained whenever possible.

After three long years of waiting, the hall was complete. It had low turf walls, the upper half of the walls being of wattle and daub. The interior was panelled in wood. These panels could be removed for replacing the turfs in the walls. Carved into the wood were animals—horned stags, snarling wolves, hovering ravens, spouting whales, and frolicking seals. The gables curved up like horns, decorated like deer. Formerly in the winter, the only light in the old hall came through the smoke hole in the ceiling or from the golden flames of fire. Now light glinted from images in the glimmering hall. The halls seemed to gleam with gold, glittering in the light of the seal oil lamps, as did the women in their coiled gold. Here glorious summer was replayed in winter. "A perversion of nature," grumbled Unferth.

Hrothgar, royal ring-breaker, stood before his people, crowded into the hall, invited to the feast after the ceremony. "My people! Today we celebrate the completion of this magnif-icent hall. Carved and golden, it robs us of speech. The only words to be spoken here are those of peace and friendship, or the plaintive song of the scop. We will call the hall 'Heorot' or 'hart' for the spirit of the wild stag, grand in his majesty yet gentle in demeanor, and for the heart of our fellowship. Let us begin the life of the hall by offering a draught to it and welcoming its presence!"

After drinking, Hrothgar continued. "I wish to thank my beloved wife, Brimhild. As you are aware, her inspiration has brought this hall about. She knows that it will reflect well on us all–not just on me as king, but on Scyldings everywhere. Her love and faith in me and this project warms my heart, just as mead glows in my bones."

Brimhild felt overjoyed at this unexpected tribute. Hrothgar, shy with his profound affection, could usually not utter it as readily as she.

"Finally, my people, I wish my son, Grendel, to stand and hold up the ceremonial cup. Let him drink first, as a sign of our faith that this building will stand for generations to come as a haven of peace and shelter for scops. Drink, my son, and then let our queen weave her web of peace amongst us."

Young Grendel drank. Brimhild received the cup from him and held it to Hrothgar's lips. She walked around the hall, first to retainers, then ladies, then farmers, fishermen, children, beggars. Two women followed her with pitchers of mead to refill the cup. Brimhild took the last sip, held up the cup and cried triumphantly, "Heorot is woven with peace."

One scop sang of all the patrons he had had. "I have served many kings, promoted peaceweavers, sung of sovereigns. I have been with the Jutes and the Jews, the Frisians and Franks, the Wylfings and Wrosnas. I have sung before Saracens, played before Persians, harped before Heathoreams. I was with Heremod. He was no kind ruler, killing comrades and butchering brothers. To me he was no indifferent king. I could tell a tale, sing a spell. For that he gave me gleaming gift, shining treasure. The leader who gives gold, praises with prizes, will not be forgotten by me. She will be shaped by scop, he will be helped by harpist." The hall laughed at the bard's boldness. Brimhild presented him with a golden collar, twisted torque. "What else can you sing for us, o wide-traveler, Widsith?"

"It is a sad song, lady, a mournful moan." The hall hubbub hushed. "The last woman of her people stood in the ashes, wept for woe, crazed with keening. No longer would her lord bestow treasure, hold hall joy, drink mead. The wreckers were wounded, heroes humbled, women made hostage, children enslaved. Their baby fingers would bleed for barbarians, boys beaten, virgins violated. Vandal victors would deny them of parents, siblings, home, and language. These would exist only in memory, precious token, revered relic. This they would shelter in the heart hoard, storing sorrow. The wavy-haired woe-wife lamented her love, grieved for her girl, bewailed her boy, pined for the past. She was the last alive, sole survivor, hating that hollow happiness."

Even the drunken men held their peace, as the glee-wood was strummed. Melancholy music faded into rafters, drifted across the land, floated over flotsam, sailed over shores, rode over realm.

Then a woman sang, made her mournful moan.

Now he is gone,
our breakwater against aliens
who wash ashore.
The flood will not ebb.

The armies come,
spilling over beaches.
Their heavy boots
sink in the sand.
They pull them

sucking out
like the wind before a storm
laying waste to the land.

The long boats
bring terror.
No one will be spared.

Tonight, the moon is full.
The tide will be high.

Unferth, bloated with beer, spoke to Brimhild. "Make sure, lady, that that woe-wife will not be you."

The hall was silent. No one knew if Unferth was joking. Brimhild felt hot. Her mouth dried up, her heart pounded. At last Hrothgar spoke. Brimhild alone saw how he grasped his dagger, his sharp-edged friend.

"You speak well, counselor. Our queen can be sure of a fine fate, festive future, with brave battlers like you to protect the land."

Unferth held his tongue. The watchers wondered if he would pull out Hrunting from his sheath, wield weapon. Massive man, he stood, walked to the throne. Unferth reached for sword, Hrothgar half stood. Then Unferth threw Hrunting onto the floor, metal clattered. Unferth knelt before his lord, his bare head almost to the floor.

Hrothgar froze, then sat down. Brimhild breathed again. This time no blood would be shed.

Then she spoke brightly to the gathering, praying for peace. "I have a riddle for you. Can you solve it?"

Gold-adorned or plain, I can be
bought or traded for various prices,
yet I am priceless.

I have a fertile pool within me if properly poked.
A thatch of flaxen hair sits atop me.
I am soft without and within,
though, when embraced by adversity,
I can grow hard.
Who am I?

One fiery fighter lowed a lascivious laugh. "Could it be my glory-twig, lady? It can grow hard!"

All the reeling revelers roared with delight. "No," answered Brimhild. At last, when no one had guessed, she answered, "A woman." She looked straight at Unferth.

Then a band of acrobats and musicians bounded in, their festive dance and song erasing the unpleasant exchange. At first Brimhild could hardly pay attention. She sat in her throne pretending to appreciate their gymnastic action. Once her blood stilled, she could beam a genuine smile at their antics. The three men and two teenaged girls tumbled and somersaulted, they danced to the piper's merry tune. One of the young women came up to Hrothgar and Brimhild at the end of their performance, while everyone in the hall applauded in a roar. The young woman had rosy cheeks from her exertion. Glowing with sweat, she had to stop talking periodically to catch her breath.

"Lady, my lord," she said, in clear and accented Danish, "we wish your hall and reign much peace and success. May we say, for joy and pleasure, our troop is always available for short or permanent hire." The hall laughed at the brazen offer. "We would make your thanes laugh at the world, not just conquer it." The king did not know how to respond to that double-edged remark.

Brimhild intervened. "My dear, your abilities are splendid indeed. You may count your performance a success. I will consider your selfless offer." Everyone laughed. "Please stay and entertain these reckless men and gentle women. For how long we will decide later."

The girl bowed and threw out her arms. Brimhild saw something flash near the girl's breast. While the king turned to his men to drink a round of mead, the queen leaned forward and called the young acrobat to her. "How old are you, my dear?"

"I don't know. I became a woman two years ago," answered the girl prettily.

Brimhild stared at the girl's face. She seemed so familiar. Yet she had never met this maid before. "Lady?" asked the girl.

"Yes?"

"Why do you look at me so?"

"I am not sure. You seem so familiar to me. Yet I am sure we never met. Where are you from?"

The girl's face darkened. "I don't remember the name of our tribe, though I still know some words of that tongue. I was too young."

"Too young for what?"

"I was enslaved, lady. The whole troop consists of slaves."

Brimhild was shocked. Of course! She had seen an older man, obviously no longer an acrobat himself, watching the troop perform. He must own them.

The girl twirled her necklace with her finger. "Don't be sad, lady. I rarely think of it anymore. After all, there are worse fates for servants. At least I can have some fun. And where would I go if I were free?"

Brimhild gazed at the girl's necklace. From it hung a single bead, dark yellow. Her mouth opened.

"Lady?" asked the girl with genuine concern. Brimhild had turned ashen.

At last she could speak. "Are you?" The girl said nothing. She seemed dumbfounded. "Are you Inga?" demanded Brimhild again, more loudly. Hrothgar turned to look at her and then the girl. He withdrew his gaze.

The girl chanted, "My name is Idun, for the goddess who

protests the golden apples of immortality for the gods."

"That bead," whispered Brimhild, almost in a moan.

"Lady, what do you know?'

"You are Inga. I knew your sister, Helga."

The girl clutched her necklace. A sob ripped out of her throat. "Where?" That single word was barely comprehensible.

"She was my friend." Brimhild began to cry. Now Hrothgar turned back, to watch carefully.

The acrobat was stricken. She couldn't talk. At last, through gasps and sobs, she uttered, "Yes, I am Inga." She fell into Brimhild's arms, which the queen had held out towards her. Then that lady had to tell Inga that her sister was dead. "She died after bearing a child. I was her best friend, and she mine." Brimhild would wait to tell some of Helga's life to the girl. She never told of Unferth's brutality.

Inga's story was not so bad, for a slave. She and the other children were taken away to the north, where the Weders ruled. The girls and boys were trained to become acrobats by the man who eventually bought them. She said she was not ill-treated, since she had to be in top physical shape to perform well and thereby earn gifts for her master. "And he does not lie with us because if we were to become pregnant, we could not perform. In fact, we are forbidden to marry."

"One day you will be too old to dance and somersault. What will happen then?"

Inga looked resigned. "Oh, then we will be killed, I imagine. For then, rather than make money, we would merely cost money."

Hrothgar watched this whole exchange with eagerness. He feared that Brimhild would reveal how Helga died. Brimhild would not betray her husband. She did, however, call the owner of the acrobats to her. He had been watching Inga with the greatest concern.

"Has Idun been bothering you, lady?" asked the man,

brusquely. Brimhild had to think for a moment and then remembered that Idun was Inga's new name. "If she has been, I will take her out and beat her happily."

"No, no," hastened Brimhild. "I wish to speak to you about her though."

His piggish eyes gleamed with anticipation. He was always one to negotiate. "Yes, lady?"

"I wish to buy her freedom from you."

The gleam intensified and then he dashed it out. He was a consumate actor. "Oh, no, lady! How could my troop survive without her? You saw for yourself what a splendid performer she is! If I lose her, I would be sure to become penniless in a matter of weeks. For who would want to see my troop without her with only these miserable wrecks to perform?" He gestured to the others who had been splendid in their vitality. The leader knew how to drive a hard bargain.

"Surely you can find a new girl and train her."

"It takes years to train a girl! And to have her fit in with this miserable lot."

"Lady," whispered Inga, "perhaps I do not want my freedom. After all, what would I do?"

"You could stay here and be free," muttered Brimhild back. She drew her attention to the owner. "What if I gave you enough gold to keep you and your troop living well for a year. Plus the purchase price of Idun."

The man was too good to be taken in by this. "Such a girl costs more now than when I bought her."

Brimhild smiled. "You are good at dealings, Hrothgar," she said, turning to her husband who had followed this exchange without a word, "you should hire this man to haggle your wergild deals. You'd save a lot of money, no doubt."

Hrothgar laughed. "My dear, just don't give up all our gold. Heorot needs to be glittering with it."

"There's nothing to worry about. I imagine this fellow will

accept my offer."

"Lady, a fair offer I have never refused."

Brimhild waved him away. "We will talk again tomorrow."

Inga came up to the queen after watching this exchange. "I don't know, my lady. The troop is my family now. They are my friends. I may be a slave, yet I never think about it. I feel like I've fashioned myself into an artist. After all, what tricks I perform, few others can rival."

Brimhild looked her in the eye. "I knew and loved your sister. My duty is to care for you. Are you telling me you want Helga's memory enshrined by your servitude? Wouldn't you like to live near your nephew, Helga's son?"

That argument was too compelling. Inga didn't have a chance to free herself from Brimhild's reasoning. No one would willingly choose slavery over freedom given the chance, would she?

Inga was an expensive friend to buy. Brimhild did it for Helga. And, it is true, Inga enjoyed being able to walk about the hall and the Scylding lands unfettered. She was free, save for her duty to Helga's memory.

Chapter 11

Uneasy Dreams

And so began a golden age for Brimhild. Her boy grew smart, quick, and brave. She loved Hrothgar and he loved her. The land thrived. Peace reigned wherever the Danish tongue was spoken. It was like the peace of Froði. That king was Odin's great-grandson. He ruled when the Emperor Augustus held sway. Froði guided Denmark in peace and triumph. No man slew another; even his father's killer went unavenged. No one robbed or stole. It was said that for three years a gold ring lay untouched on the main road over the moor.

This could not last long. Froði was soon killed.

Secretly Brimhild presented Grendel with the ways of Christ. She admitted she did not know if such a man existed. Neither had she seen Odin. "It is all a matter of faith, my son. Only you can choose your way. One day, you will be king and you must decide the faith best for your people."

The seasons passed. Hrothulf, Hrothgar's nephew, son of Halga now dead, became their foster child. His and Grendel's presence could not assuage her desire for another child of her own. Brimhild became pregnant once more, only to birth bloody bits after a few months. Ælfsciene, crippled crone, had been dead several years. The queen had to prepare by herself the dried hare's heart, worked into dust, and a third part of frankincense powder, drinking them in clear wine for seven days. She took three new sprouts of pennyroyal, those with the strongest scent, pounded into old wine, to drink. Twice a day Brimhild drank brooklime boiled in milk and in water. To heal her insides, she mingled wolf's milk with wine and honey in like quantities.

Brimhild called the dead child Maria Lunae, Mary of the Moon, for she loved the Madonna for her maternal love. The moon was a beautiful land of milky mystery that beckoned to her. After the child had been buried, she took dirt from the baby's grave. This she wrapped up in black wool and sold to a merchant. Then she said, "You buy, I sell, this grim stuff and this grain of grief."

She visited her parents, aged and ailing. They had saved her, an innocent child. They, in their wisdom, raised her to respect Scylding tradition and the power of the gods. Fate called their failing bodies to Niflheim. They sank into ceaseless sleep.

At this time, they were visited by a foreign fighter, young Geat. He presented himself at court, bid Hrothgar's mercy. "I am Ecgtheow, exiled from enemies. I slew Heatholaf, warrior of the Wylfings. I seek your help, want wergild, a diplomat for peace. Can you, Hrothgar, lord of the Scyldings, save my people from enemy reprisals? I come to you in desperation, ask aid. Shape a treaty, and my people will be in your debt. Later, you may call on the Geats for support, vanquish vandals, banish barbarians."

Hrothgar sought counsel. The men agreed that having the Geats obliged to the Scyldings was no bad thing. "Though," said Unferth, "what if the Franks or Swedes wipe out the Geats before we can use them? They are not so strong a tribe."

Later, those enemies would rejoice after Ecgtheow's son died. Often Unferth spoke rashly. This would not be one of those times.

Brimhild stayed at Heorot to rule, sat on gift-stool. Hrothgar brought a small party with him to the Wylfings. That short voyage was no trial for the longboat. Hrothgar, Healfdene's son, lord of the Honor-Danes, spoke to Helm. Hrothgar promised fine treasures, twisted gold, gleaming gems. The Scyldings and Wylfings built a bargain, crafted compact. Impressed with Hrothgar's generosity, Helm gave him a prize for peace, present for posterity.

Hrothgar brought home this foreign captive. Wealhtheow, lady of the Helmings, younger than Brimhild, came to be his woman. Brimhild retained possession of the household keys on her belt at her waist, signifying her position as first wife. Hrothgar visited her seldom after the arrival of his fair young concubine. Like Sif, wife of Thor, Wealhtheow boasted a mane of wonderful golden hair, like sheaves of wheat, fertile shafts. She bore him one daughter and two sons.

One day, on the mead-path procession from the ladies' hall, Wealhtheow said to Brimhild, "You, lady, may be the first to win our lord's heart. I am the one to retain it. My sons will come to sit on the gift-stool."

Brimhild answered, "Hrothgar's heir is Grendel. He is the first-born. And I wear the keys to this household."

"That may be. Hrothgar sleeps with me out of desire, with you out of duty."

Like Gudrun and Brynhild at the bath, like Freya and Hyndla on their way to Valhalla, these women made swordplay of wordplay. Hyndla called Freya a she-goat in heat, no faithful wife to her wanderer husband. Gudrun told Brynhild her husband, Gunnar, was no man. One was a helm tree, the other a shield tree, the hall was a wolf-forest, their glances a hail of arrows, their words dripped with dew of wounds. A shared husband causes much spindle strife, wife woe.

The hall, too, was no longer a dam of delight, mere of merriment. The idle fighters, prisoners of peace, were indolent and violent, attacking one another at the slightest provocation since the still silence was like a pestilence. They ate and slept and drank. The work of home, field, and sea was left to crones, withered greybeards, and men scornful of the ways of the hall. Ale was a brew of truth, causing waggle-tongued warriors to blurt out harshly about long-past transgressions. These sickening slogans were cured only with steel and the shedding of blood. They played at dice and cut in defiance of cheating. No happy heroes were these beneath the golden roof, shining with shame.

Brimhild made one last attempt to retain her husband. She

spoke her lament. "Where is the love you once bore me? Where is the babe we held? Where are the arms you embraced me with? Where is the desire you once sparked in me and I in you? Where is the understanding of one another? Where is the pity? Where is the joy? Where is the past? Where is my place?"

Hrothgar looked at her sadly. "I loved you—you were so mysterious and beautiful. I wanted to understand you."

Brimhild replied, "You wanted to own me. You wanted to take possession of me just as you raid villages. Do you understand the people you rob and rape? Do you understand me? Look at this hall! I've made your reputation. You are known throughout the grey salt sea because of me—the scops we paid, the hall I've built."

Hrothgar's compassion was spent. "You want us to control conquered people with art and pretty songs, music and hall building. We can only control violent forces with brutality and force. Who paid for that hall? The more you built, the more I had to raid to pay for it. This hall is paid for in blood—it's red gold which covers it, not just the red of gleaming and burnished metal—the red of blood."

Brimhild understood he was right. The glory and the beauty were only made possible by death and violence.

That gold-burnished hall was not yet red from tongues of flame.

One night Unferth whispered to the scop. The thane made an announcement. "Now we will hear how Brynhild sang of her sore straights, her plight of passion."

The harpist held up his instrument, strummed the strings.

Unferth looked at Brimhild as this song pierced the hall. Like Brynhild, she lost her beloved to another. Her heart was striken. Unferth was no breeder of peace.

Chapter 12

Dance with Me

Thirty half-years old, Grendel grew into a fine youth, slim as a reed, and sweet as honey. Yet this son was no source of constant joy as before. His father took him on a raiding party to initiate him into manhood. When he returned, he would not tell his mother what had happened. A rift had been created between father and son.

"He is soft," scoffed Hrothgar, king of the Victory-Scyldings. "How can he ever be king if he does not follow our ways of conquering other peoples?"

"I wish I were just a farmer, Father! Then I could tend to my own business and family. Your way of life shatters Scyldings, fights family, hates home."

Brimhild felt helpless to reconcile them. The loving boy seemed to her to be in the right.

Inga was a consolation in this time of unhappiness. She was a merry girl, prattling about the many courts she had visited and the funny antics she and her fellow acrobats had gotten up to. "Once, before the Heathobards, Bragi dropped me during a stunt. I clonked my head on the hard dirt floor of the hall. The king shouted out, 'I pay good money for bunglers?' I thought he was going to hit us. Then Bragi said, 'You fell, Idun, just as we practiced it. Even the king thought it was an accident.' No one said anything. I was terrified. Then one thane laughed, then another, and another, until the whole hall reverberated. Still I was glad to leave that play area."

The dancer Idun, born to the name Inga, was comforted to hear of Helga, though Brimhild concealed much of Helga's sadness from her sister. Inga never spoke of the time her mother died and she was captured. Brimhild didn't dare ask.

One day Brimhild had asked Inga to help her with the weaving. They met in the loom room of one of the outbuildings. Inga was singing a jolly little ditty that she danced to. Brimhild hadn't noticed that her foster-child, Hrothulf, Hrothgar's nephew, had entered the room some time earlier. He said nothing, only looked at Inga. He was a very serious youth. Brimhild never saw him smile. Inga, who did not notice him, asked Brimhild, "Do you like my little dance? Perhaps I should perform it tonight. It might make the hall a jollier place. It's been so dismal of late."

"Lady," broke in Hrothulf. Inga jumped at the sound of his voice. Brimhild just continued weaving.

"Yes, Hrothulf?" asked the queen calmly. She had never been close to the boy, who seemed still to be in mourning for his father, Hrothgar's brother, who had been dead for years.

"The king wishes to know if you would serve the cup tonight," he said solemnly.

"What an honor," exclaimed Inga sarcastically. "After all, she only bore him his first-born son and is his proper queen. How kind of him to allow her to do so and not his whore." Inga was still hurting at Hrothgar's betrayal of Brimhild.

"Inga! Do not speak so. The king is within his rights to do as he chooses," pointed out Brimhild.

"Yes. Still, he exceeds the custom of nobility," Inga retorted.

Hrothulf turned red in the face. He managed to sputter out, "Who are you to condemn the king? His grace freed you."

"The true queen freed me, not him. Why do you defend him, anyway? After all, your father was the older brother. Why aren't you king?" asked Inga.

The girl knew she had gone too far. She typically would be childlike and gay, then say something she immediately regretted and plead for forgiveness. Although fully in control when performing, she lost all measure when she spoke in private. Petulant and pert, she knew no bounds of propriety.

Hrothulf turned icy and ignored the girl. He turned again to the queen. "Lady?"

Brimhild calmly continued to weave. "Tell him I will be there," she replied.

Once Hrothulf left, Brimhild turned on the girl in fury. "You know perfectly well that Halga died long ago when Hrothulf was only a baby. Of course he couldn't be king. Hrothgar may not be a perfect husband. But he has kept our kingdom free from enemies."

"You say this, Brimhild? I have heard how you defied him about all sorts of things, including slavery. And yet you tell me he is the epitome of the good lord?"

"Don't turn on me because you made an error in judgment, speaking as you did. I want you to apologize to Hrothulf."

"I won't!" refused Inga.

"You will," said Brimhild icily.

Inga came over to her mistress and hugged her. Tears came into Inga's eyes. "I'm sorry," the girl said pitifully.

Brimhild continued to weave, then put the shuttle down. She hugged Inga. "You are like a daughter to me. I just want to see you be your best."

"I'll say I'm sorry," she promised.

Later that week Inga saw Hrothulf outside gathering hay into sheaves. She approached him. He looked up, saw who it was, then looked away. His forbidding expression did not change.

Inga began to hum. She then did a little dance. She chanted a child's song.

Hrothulf did not glance up. He continued to gather hay into bundles, then sat down, facing toward the sea, away from her.

"Hrothulf." His shoulders stiffened for a moment. "I'm sorry. I shouldn't have said that. About you not being king."

His muscles relaxed. He didn't reply. He returned to his work.

"Brimhild told me I was wrong and had to apologize. I would have come and said I was sorry anyway. I knew I was wrong."

Hrothulf tied up a bundle with some thin rope. The wind blew from the sea. Then Inga heard his voice. "You weren't wrong."

"Oh, yes, I was," she gushed. "I know I was. I never think before I speak. I never reflect. I'm always jumping into things before giving a moment's thought. I suppose I'm an acrobat with how I speak, tumbling and then getting back up again, barely balancing."

"You were right, I said." This time Inga held her tongue. "You were right." Hrothulf still would not look at her. He stopped his work. The sea drew his gaze. "I should be king. How do you think it feels to be obligated to someone you feel should not be king. How do you think I feel to be duty-bound to my uncle, my foster-father? I am indebted to him, yet I resent him. Who am I in all this? Who am I? Why can't I act? Why don't I act?" He spoke so quietly she wasn't sure of what she heard. At his last question, though, he turned to look her directly in the eye. He had piercing blue ones. She felt a chill. For once, she was speechless. Then he went back to work. "You are a child, Inga. Stay that way. It is the only protection in this world."

She felt uncertain and scared, so left him working. She turned to give him one last look before she disappeared into the hall.

A few weeks later Inga performed in the hall for a visiting group of allies from Sweden. She wore a blue gown, which clung to her as she sang and danced to a melody from the White Sea. Everyone clapped when she was through. Then general dancing began. Brimhild was not present at this occasion, since Wealhtheow had been called upon to preside. Inga made her way to the back of the hall to join her friend, the queen, in the women's quarters.

"Inga!" someone called before she could leave the hall. She turned around. It was Hrothulf.

She stood and felt nervous. Why did he call for her now? He seemed to have accepted her apology the other day. He hadn't given her a single glance since then. It takes much strength for a man to pretend to be looking in the opposite direction when his secret beloved comes into the room, secret even from himself.

She looked up at him. Those burning eyes smoldered still. He frightened her.

"What do you want?" she finally asked. "I was going to see the true queen."

Hrothulf didn't hush her, even though Wealhtheow could have heard. He couldn't hear anything save his own blood rushing through his veins. The music the scop played was lively and gay. Inga felt oppressed somehow. Her face grew flush and hot. As he said nothing, she turned to go.

"Dance with me," he blurted out.

"What?" she asked, turning back.

"Dance with me." His tongue felt ten times too large for his mouth.

Inga kept her serious countenance. Suddenly, like the sun bursting through clouds, she grinned. She held out her hands. Hrothulf, half-stunned, couldn't move. She came up to him and took his hands, then led him in the jig. Hrothulf was smiling by the end of it, in embarassment at his incompetence and in utter adoration of his goddess.

Chapter 13

Will We Burn?

"Lady," Hrothulf said to Inga, "come to the beach with me."

Inga, who trusted Hrothulf, went to the sea in the late afternoon, as the sun was about to set. There in the wet sand, runes were written.

"I cannot read them," confessed Inga.

"I shall read them to you." Hrothulf hesitated, finally speaking.

It's strange
not to touch
the one you love.

You are on one island,
I on another.
What joins us?

Nothing can part us,
because we are not together.

Will we burn?
I do.

As he read, the tide came in and crumbled the words—not the emotion. Inga's heart pondered. Like light filtering through the smoke hole of the roof's hall, she allowed love to creep into a crack in her heart. The water of desire rushed through that crack and made it a fissure, then a gorge. And the water gushed through.

Inga spoke in response.

I don't want
my fantasies to come true now,
but in some safe and distant future,
when your fair hand
can caress me
and I can touch you back,
now avoiding only
the desire
which haunts us,
fearing only
the desire consuming us.

It was understood that they, in their desire, would never touch. He could never betray her intention to remain pure.

Once, Hrothulf held Inga's hand. She did not want him to, yet she could not stop him. She could not stop herself.

While he didn't believe the God of Jerome, he was stirred to think of that religion. To Inga, he confessed,

Jesus's touch could heal.
He'd cure the ill,
help the lame to walk,
the blind to see.
Our touch is sacred too.
I am healed,
I glow with health,
I shine with beatitude,
I am transfigured
when your hands hold mine.

She refused to let him hold her fingers. Not touching became as erotic, no, more so, than the stroke of flesh on flesh. So argued Hrothulf, not without regret,

God knows we are no saints,
yet our salvation lies
in our denial.
From our restraint
comes grace.
If this is how it feels
to be no saint,
let us be saints,
without denial,
without restraint,
without control.

Inga replied,

Restraint is the visible sign of our love.
Our holding back
fills us with grace.

Chapter 14

The Loyal Thane

After many years abroad, Jerome returned from his pilgrimage. He did not come back alone.

The night of his return, all the retainers gathered in the hall. Brimhild was permitted to preside on this occasion. Grendel sat between his parents. Jerome entered the hall. Hrothgar rose to greet him.

"Dear friend, your absence of many half-years has saddened us. Nothing can cheer us more than your return. We may have quarreled in the past. Let us be brothers, one and all, in the days which come."

Brimhild rose. She presented the cup to Hrothgar who drank, then to Grendel who rose to make his first speech as a man. "Dear Uncle, for so I see you, your presence has been missed here among us. You bring us new ways of thought. I drink to the willingness of this court to hear the best of the world's beliefs that we can then use to our advantage. We should not reject a new faith because we fear our own inadequate."

At this, Unferth reddened in anger. Brimhild walked to Jerome, presented him with the cup. "This chalice," said Jerome, "is not unlike one shared by Christ and his apostles. Let our brotherhood be so strong."

"I thought there was a traitor," muttered Unferth.

"Yes, brother, there was. No man would betray an honest gesture or a heartfelt deed in this hall, would he?"

Unferth shook with rage.

Brimhild held the cup aloft before the court. "I bid my lord and husband to continue this fine reign by asking all men and women of any faith to be made welcome here. For a strong realm can withstand any headwind. In fact, it speeds along the voyage of the ring-carved prow." She drank from the cup and sat.

"My lord Hrothgar," said Jerome, rising, "I have a happy task to perform. I did not return alone from my journey. I brought this woman."

From the women's quarters a tall figure came forth. Over a hundred half-years old, she bowed to Hrothgar and his queen.

"Who is this lady? Your wife?" teased Hrothgar. "I thought your priests forswore soft flesh."

The court laughed.

"No, king," said Jerome, smiling at the jest, "it is a woman of your realm, formerly the land of the Jutes."

"Indeed. And who may you be?"

"May I speak first?" asked Jerome.

"If you wish."

"As the court knows, our beloved queen Brimhild was carried to our country on the gannet's bath from across the sea. No one knew who she was. Only that her kindly parents found her, loved her, and raised her as their own. Before I left on my wandering, the queen graced me with certain knowledge. She showed me two objects present in her cradleboat — a spoon and a book. The spoon I determined to be a Christian baptismal spoon and the book the Christian Gospel."

The court was noisy with shock and wonderment.

Hrothgar spoke over the hubbub, verging on anger. "Why did you not tell me, Brimhild?"

"A traitor indeed!" said Unferth.

"My lord and husband, loving retainers and dear ladies, I said nothing of this because I thought Jerome might never return. My origins are unclear as ever. It is true — I must have been baptized as a child."

The court again was a noisy hive of questions.

Jerome spoke, his voice hushing the tumult. "Your birth, my lady, is a mystery I have endeavored to solve. And the answer is here." He gestured to the lady guest.

The woman stood before the king, the queen, and their child. The queen spoke at last, her voice trembling. "Who are you, lady?"

"I am Fara, daughter of Sigbert, of the people of the Jutes."

"You are welcome to our home. What do you know of my birth? All I know was told to me by my parents. My mother discovered me washed ashore in a woven boat, created as a kind of cradle. The woman who found me became my mother, her husband my father. Though dead, I love them as my own flesh and blood."

"Sixty half-years ago, I put a girl child named Sif in such a boat," said Fara. "I kissed her forehead and her sweet lips and watched the tide carry her over the horizon to a foreign shore. I left her with several leather skins filled with milk, with dried fish and bread, and some valuable objects of our family, Christian treasure given to us from our leader. After I lost sight of her cradle on the horizon, the Heathobards attacked our village, as our lookout had warned. My husband was slaughtered in the battle. I and my only other child, a boy older than the babe, were taken into slavery. My boy child died of disease when we were sold to Huns. Only ten half-years ago did I find freedom and return to my home. I waited in my village to hear word of my lost daughter. One day, this good priest," she pointed to Jerome, "came. He stayed many days, teaching us of Christ, whose love I had discovered as a girl. He asked if anyone had lost a child by sea. And so I told him what I knew."

Brimhild could not see. Light glinted off the watery joy in the wells of her eyes. Brimhild cried shimmering mists at the discovery of her mother, just as Freya had cried tears of red gold at the loss of her husband. Fara continued to speak. "I told this priest I had to set my child on the mercy of the waves. He said it coincided with your arrival here, o queen."

Brimhild arose and held out her arms. "Mother, come rest your head on my bosom, as I once laid mine on yours. Stay forever here at peace." The regal dame encased her mother in her embrace. The court was greatly moved. After they kissed, Brimhild introduced her mother to all gathered present. "My mother, Fara, daughter of Sigbert, of the Jutes. She shall remain a member of our clan and realm from henceforth." Then Brimhild held up the ceremonial cup and presented it to her mother. "O venerable sage mother, teach me of your ways so that I may love and honor them and you." Fara drank.

Then Brimhild presented the cup to Hrothgar, Grendel, Æschere the rune counselor, Wolfgar the herald and chamberlain, Hrothulf son of Halga, and Unferth and Jerome, Ecglaf's sons.

One evening in the hall, the king, queen, her mother, Jerome, Unferth, and Æschere sat drinking mead. Wealhtheow was in her bairns' bedroom, caring for children, blood kin to the king.

Fara shared with them the lament she had sung in the years following the loss of her daughter.

Brimhild stood up and embraced her mother. "Now I can hold on to you and my past." Fara smiled at her grown child.

Then a player plaited the plight of Hildeburh, doleful woman of Finnsburh.

'Here lies my brother,
king of the Danes,
king of his people,
king of my people.
Killed by the enemy
killed by the Frisians,
killed by my people.

Here lies my son,
prince of the Frisians,
prince of his people,

prince of my people.
Killed by the enemy,
killed by the Danes,
killed by my people.

Who are my people?
Where is my home?
In the land of my roots
or of my blossoms?
With the men of my father
or those of my husband?

At least my man lives,
Finn, king of the Frisians.
Peace-gold will be offered.
My grief will find solace
in the end of blade play.'

She did not yet know
the new Danish king
would lift the brightest of swords
to slay her shining warrior.
She will return home,
her silhouette dark
against the golden flames
of the pyre.

A melancholy mood dejected them. To break it, Hrothgar asked Fara to tell them of the royal habits of the Jutes. After she did so, Jerome told about threats to destroy Rome from barbarians. During his absence, he heard many rumors of warriors from the east who intended to sack that great city.

Brimhild spoke. "Tell me, Mother, if you can, more of my family. Who was my father?"

"My husband was a fisherman when he was not counseling our lord. That's how he could make the cradleboat. The lookout told of a raiding party. That's why we left you on the whale's back. I wished no slavery for you. Our son we kept with us as he was older, twelve half-years. He insisted on remaining to fight as a man, although his father had also made a boat for him to escape in. He remained to die a slave, ill and wracked in pain."

"What was my father's name?"

Fara looked at Brimhild, then into the firelight. "I do not know," she finally said.

"Mother!" said Hrothgar in shocked surprise. "How could you not know your husband's name?"

"Brimhild's father was not my husband." Her listeners held their breath.

"Mother?" Brimhild was filled with fear.

"Five half-years before I had to leave you to the waves' mercy, we were attacked by pirates. They were Scyldings."

"There are many Scyldings," said Unferth darkly.

"Indeed. That day there seemed no end of them. My husband was out fishing. He and his friends journeyed early to a good fishing ground near Ireland. He was gone for two months. My boy, Ethelwald, and I were at home. Our village is a fishing port. Most husbands were gone. We lived only a half day's journey on foot from our lord. There had been no warning. The longships were drawn up on the beach, the heavy footsteps of men crashed through the waves and crunched the sand. I hid Ethelwald in a chest, before one wild-haired, bearded Scylding entered my home.

"I was terrified, fearful that your brother would cry. The man uttered words I did not understand, questioning I think where our valuables were. I gestured to a basket—in there were some gold coins. My husband had taken the other gold pieces to use in trading. The Scylding seemed angered that was all I had and demanded for more in his gutteral way. My heart stopped.

"Out of the corner of my eye, I saw the chest lid rise. Ethelwald's bright eye gleamed, watching. The man then shoved me back with his gloved hands, hard gloves with spikes they were. A drop of blood from my breast fell to the floor, hard and caked with dirt. He removed his gloves slowly and threw them on the bed. I stared at his hands, mesmerized by their power, their strength, their menace. Then I fell back and—" She could not finish. Tears streamed down Brimhild's face. The men did not speak.

A shadow moved against the wall of Heorot.

Fara said then, "I knew my child was his, not my husband's since he had been away at sea. Ethelwald saw it all. He never spoke after that day until the moment he died. As his fever caused sweat to dampen his brow, I know he was ashamed he failed me then. Yet, when it happened, he had only been eight half-years old!" Fara cried and Brimhild held her.

"When my husband returned, I told him what had happened, of course. I could not deny the pregnancy. I prayed to lose this barbarian's child. Then, Brimhild, I knew I had to love you, as you were innocent. A sweet girl. I loved you tenderly. And I accepted you as a member of our family. You see, my husband had discovered Christ and knew your soul was clean as was mine. Ethelwald never knew that your real father was that Dane."

"If I knew who he was," muttered Brimhild, "I would kill him."

"Now, now, my child, you are here because of him, too, remember?"

"What can I tell Grendel?" The shadow against the wall hesitated, clung to the darkness.

"Nothing, my wife," said Hrothgar, "why does he need to know?"

"Because he should see that such rapacious pirate parties damage innocent people's lives."

"He already knows that," Jerome assured her.

"Yes, all too well," said Brimhild regretfully.

"Indeed," said Hrothgar ruefully, "bloodshed is not Grendel's path."

"Would you ever know this Dane again?" asked Brimhild.

"Not by face," Fara assured her. "He was dressed in the Scylding fashion, his hair and beard were wild. He had already been out raiding for some time. All I know is that he wore a golden ring on those massive fingers."

"A ring?" asked Æschere suddenly.

"It looked like this." Fara drew the shape of Thor's hammer in the dirt of the floor. "I shall never forget it."

All those with her stared at the pattern. "Nor I," whispered Brimhild hollowly. "Was this it?" she asked, pulling the chain up around her neck to reveal the hammer ring presented to her on her wedding night.

"Yes, but how—?" asked Fara. She looked at Hrothgar, who had already risen, his dagger drawn. Sudden recognition flooded in her eyes.

"No!" screamed Brimhild.

Jerome moved toward Fara and Brimhild. The only weapon carried by this warrior for Jesus was the golden cross hanging around his neck.

He then hung from that gallows, strangled by his brother, Unferth, kin to Cain. Christ's apostle was dead.

Unferth turned to Fara who screamed in terror. His sword stopped that voice. Unferth approached Brimhild, determined to finish her, his royal nemesis.

Unferth was a loyal thane.

Hrothgar had sought out the shadowy figure in his hall, determined to prevent this news from spreading. Brimhild caught sight of her son, moving from the shadows where he had lurked, innocently eavesdropping, listening to that woeful tale. She leapt onto Hrothgar, who shoved her aside.

"You begot me?" she whispered. "You married me!"

Hrothgar almost pierced her body with his iron friend. He could hear people coming to the hall, roaring with the din of death. He hesitated and lowered his weapon. "Take her away! And the boy! I never want to see them again," commanded Hrothgar.

Unferth and Æschere grabbed her arms. "Mother!" Brimhild cried repeatedly, until her voice was hoarse. "Mother!"

Grendel leapt on the men as they dragged Brimhild outside. They managed to push off the young man and toss him onto the ground. They returned to flank their lord.

Hrothgar's frame was outlined in the doorway, looking out at them. "Never return!" he commanded. "You both are banished on pain of death." Like the ice-covered lake, that king was frozen and hard.

"Father!" cried Grendel. The door shut behind the men. "Grandfather!"

Mother and son stood beneath a moonless, cloudy sky. Winter's fingers caressed their bare necks and faces. A curlew cried her lament. The rime-fettered ground was no comfort bed to them. They wandered off, journeying as aliens in a foreign land.

This once happened; so, too, this will pass.

III. The Mere-Wife

A wonder happened: the sea turned to bone.

Old English Riddle 69

One day you'll fight, my son. I pray you battle the open sea, waxing waves, and not the armor-clad warrior. The warrior, seasoned soldier, knows death as his lover, fears not the bloody sword, grips the unwilling woman, learns to hate. May you choose the homely croft. Here vegetables grow to feed your many children. The sea is a teeming treasury, not of booty and gold, but of meat, oil, and clothing. Scorn not the simple life, far from the hall, haven from hostility. Love the homeland, the hearth, the humble stable. The breath of animals will warm you at night, not the hot red juice of the vanquished foe. The arms of a woman desiring you will cling around your shoulders, not the terrified scratches of a captive.

Stay here, my son, don't yearn for exile from home.

Yet I fear you'll leave. Young men always do.

Chapter 15

The Alone-Goer

A. D. 412, by the mere in Scylding land

Aunt Ælfsciene's cottage was a shambles, abandoned as it had been for many years. It was the only shelter Brimhild knew of. Her parents' home had long been taken over by a fisherman and his family. They dared not endanger anyone in the realm with the disease of exile. The cottage lay half a day's journey distant. They travelled in darkness and grim chill, speaking no words. What could Brimhild say? Grendel had heard all. There would be plenty of time for speech. Exile was a sea of words creating warm memories in the chill of the solitary soul, lost and frightened after crossing the border of society into frozen rejection.

Ælfsciene had lived by the fens and marshes, a viscous wasteland, neither firm ground nor liquid sea. The reeds betokened land and solid substance, while the ground was wet and muddy. Bog holes could swallow a man in moments. Quicksand burbled threateningly. Ælfsciene abided on the border of known lands, neither land nor water, because she existed as neither woman nor man. She rejected the marriage of Danish custom, yet did not gird her loins as a man. She practiced the secrets of ancient lore and frightened men with her power, living with the border creatures. Eels were her retainers, water-serpents her court ladies, ravens her messengers, wolves her friends. In this grim place, she had made her home.

Shading the mere was an oak, struck by Thor's lightning. This was no World Tree. That tree feeds the hart, whose milk becomes shining mead, never drying up, quenching the warriors of Valhalla. In that place, a goat bites off the buds, teats run with mead, filling a never empty cauldron. That tree's fruit are fed to women who labor, so that what is within may pass out.

This tree blocked out the sun, twisted branches silhouetted against the storm clouds, heralding drear dread.

Now the exiles, alien and banished, came to this borderland. They waited for sun up to cross the bog, whose bright green hummocks could lead to a death grip by melted sand-glue. The hut had been knocked down by the wind and snows of many years. Some tools of rusted iron lay on the ground. Dried herbs flew into the wind, carried out over the marshy grave. The hovel lay by the tarn, teeming with sea creatures. The mere offered peat as fuel and building material. Grendel cut the black turf from which they forged low walls. They traveled to the forests for twigs to weave wicker walls, high up from the earth. They labored with hands that once had woven the web of peace countless times, but now were calloused in cobbling together a shelter in no man's—no woman's land. They drank brackish water, ate dried fish, and cooked lake-lichen. Here was no honeyed mead hall in this haven of desperation and despair. They grimly held on, confused, bewildered, and bitter.

One night Grendel went to Heorot to confront his father-grandfather, to ask him why and how it should be? To plead with him to pity his mother, to bestow his fatherhood back on his son. Grendel was a striking youth, flaxen-haired, shining with golden spirit and courage. He journeyed at twilight to his father's hall. Heorot, built in Brimhild's honor, again echoed with merriment and joy once the pollution of Grendel and his mother had been purified by Wealhtheow's perfume.

The scop sang. The harp hummed of earth's creation.

"Fire and ice collided, created a frost ogre, shaped like man. His name was Ymir. When he slept, one leg fucked the other. A son was crafted from that loathsome love-making, putrid penetration, corrupt copulation. All his kin were evil. From him are descended all ill-tempered trolls and evil elves. Grendel and his mother come from this stock.

"When the frost thawed, a cow appeared. Her teats fed Ymir with miraculous milk. Then she licked ice-blocks. Inside was a man, handsome and brave. He married the daughter of giants, fine folk. Their son was Odin. He killed Ymir, making the world from that corpse. The sea and lakes are his blood, the earth is his flesh, the mountains his bones, the rocks and pebbles his teeth and broken bones. That was a good killing!"

The men chuckled. Hidden outside, Grendel listened to this creation chronicle, felt bitter at heart. Even the poet exiled him from the religion of redemption.

Finally all the warriors lay asleep on the benches. Grendel entered Heorot.

"Who's there?" a rough voice cried.

"It is I, a friend."

"What friend?" asked another.

"The son of the king."

"His sons sleep with their nursemaids, they are no men."

"I am his son, here to claim the privilege of speech with my father."

Grendel heard swords removed from their scabbards. He slowly removed his.

"You must leave, Grendel. You are the spawn of a lustful adulteress, her bastard boy."

"Bastard? I? She is no faithless wife. Who told you that?"

"After your exile, we all knew. You are the child of that Christian priest and that witch and traitor. A wolf often sleeps in the son of an outlaw."

So, too, in the gods' hall were such accusations made. Loki, part man, part woman, told Freya she was a whore. She slept with everyone in the hall, so Loki proclaimed before them all. The gods found her in her brother's bed when she farted. Skathi, Freyr's stepmother, and Sif, Thor's wife, were said to have begged Loki to share their beds, so Loki proclaimed. Poisonous words led to Loki's torture, poison dripped on his body, searing snake, burning balm.

Grendel denied the false flyting, rotten wrongs. "No! It isn't so!"

"Your mother is lucky. In ancient days such a wife would be stripped, her hair laid bare. She would be turned out of her home publicly and flogged through the village. Hrothgar is merciful. We defend him, Lord of the Spear-Danes. Leave or we must kill you. The orders have been given."

Grendel paused. "I cannot leave without my rights being heard."

"You may not approach the gift-stool, the treasure throne."

Swords struck out. Grendel, whose tender heart made him weak in raids, had been trained by the best of swordsmen, weapon-wielders. His sword answered back, severing the bone rings of one stout warrior. The other bore upon him, laying on him, his stiff weapon almost slicing him. At last Grendel ducked away and wielded his sword swiftly through the air, cutting a throat in a warm burst of blood. He heard footsteps. "Who goes there?" All at once, several men approached. Grendel slipped into the black chill, back along the moor. His time must wait.

Grendel returned from that first night, sticky blood matting his golden curls. Bloodshed promised a vow of never ending violence, a cycle of revenge ending only in exhaustion or forgetting. Brimhild wept to think of her own child denied his proper place. Her own loss she could bear, just not his unjust exile. Like Baldr, secretly sprung from celestial seed, Grendel was as beautiful as ivory inlaid in oak, his hair lovelier than gold. White flowers are likened to Baldr's brow. Grendel's glory was great. Yet he became an alone-goer, outlaw wolf.

Grendel tried, time and again, to meet his father and speak with that king. Many a fine warrior died for this desire and his father's command. The retainers took to sleeping in outbuildings and barns for fear of this sole boy. Hrothgar himself fled to the women's quarters, rooster among hens.

Chapter 16

Islands Adrift

Inga sang in the hall as Hrothulf passed by. She whispered a little song,

You are on one island,
I on another.

Would he remember? Yes, he would. That night Hrothulf came to the beach where he had once written runes. "Come away with me," urged Hrothulf. "Now I would leave this place."

Inga sadly shook her head. "I cannot leave while Brimhild stays exiled. Grendel refuses to go. He wants to be king one day."

Hrothulf drew in his breath. "That will never happen."

"I know," she whispered. "Yet I cannot leave them."

"I understand." Hrothulf looked infinitely sad. "Then I must stay with Hrothgar, and persuade him not to slaughter them. They easily could be killed, you know."

Hrothulf did what he had never dared do before. He held her face tenderly between his hands to gently kiss her mouth. Taking hold of her hand, he held briefly held it to his breast and walked desolately away.

One day, Inga sang before the guests in the hall. All heard her poignant song and saw her languid dance, meant for Hrothulf alone.

The Danish landscape,
emerges from the dingle's shelter,
onto the fierce fell,
scrambles along screes,
makes passage across open moors

covered in scratchy heath,
avoids fluorescent bogs, alluring pits of death,
drinks the wintery juice of the icy burn
beckoning
loud in the silence of the waste,
it bites teeth,
quenches and hurts.
The cheating sea
lures us to its chill touch.

Grey and grey and grey.
Never fixed,
shifting, constantly wavering,
shimmering colors which cannot be pinned down
(like your eyes).

The mist envelops us.
We hear the slap of sea-roughened waves
on weedy skerry,
seal's song.
Is it the selkie,
a seal-woman, who once a year
sheds her skin becoming human?
If you find her skin,
you can keep her with you forever.
But if she finds it,
she must return to the sea,
no matter how much she loves you.

Have you hidden my skin
in your heart?
Then I will never find it,
I can never leave,
for we are one.

We cling to the shore —
this grim splendor
this braw beauty
this harsh heaven
this tide pool of dreams,
jagged, cutting shells, and limpid spray.

'Twixt land and sea,
I perch,
only at home
on the limen shore,
at the briny brink,
sinking into the threshold sand
as the bordering tide pulls at me,
in and out,
as it ebbs and floods.

Hrothulf sang under his breath.

You speak.
My heart stops
to listen.

Chapter 17

The Wanderer

The prospect from the steps of the great hall looked down over the heath to a long slope, across to the shingle and sandy beach and, at last, the ocean itself. The time it took to reach the salt waves on foot equaled the time it took to quaff a horn of mead, if you stopped to make a coarse joke or two while drinking. It was mid-afternoon and the sun was soon to set. The wind whipped up whitecaps. Spray flew across the dull brown heath. The clouds were grey and low, the light dim as when seal oil lamps smoked.

The girl wrapped her cloak tightly around her as she stooped over the steps, sweeping sand, dirt, and debris onto the ground. It seemed a useless task, the wind as easily could carry junk to the steps as away. This was her task, even though she was the daughter of the overlord, the king. He believed his children should perform all kinds of work to gain the respect of their followers. She was only a girl and did not yet feel that cleaning was a form of drudgery. No, she merely obeyed her father's wishes, wishes resisted by her mother. She only meant to be on the stoop for a few moments, as long as it would take to clear the entrance of filth. Sometimes, she would look out to the sea that beckoned every eye that stood at this spot. The gleaming sun-bright sea. The whale-path was the source of their wealth and the home of their destruction. She wished to cross the breakers as men did, traveling to far-off lands, conquering distant peoples, encountering strange customs.

One day, she would travel in a long ship, a journey that would not promise joy. That would not take place until she had grown into a young woman.

Just before she turned to go back inside she caught a

movement out of the corner of her eye. Down near the shore, hunched over and making its way slowly, carefully, was a small figure in grey, hobbling with a twisted cane. It barely seemed to move, so slowly it went. Deliberately it approached the hall, over the heathland. A stranger, she thought. She waited.

Finally the shriveled figure came to the bottom of the steps. The grey cloak covered his head and he looked out at her from the darkness of his veil. "Can an old man rest for the night here, maiden?"

"I will ask," the girl answered. She shot indoors, letting her broom clatter onto the outside steps. "Father! Mother!" They were conferring near the giftstool where her father held court.

"Yes, my dear?" said her mother.

"A stranger asks to spend the night."

Her father stood up in alarm.

The girl laughed. "He is no danger. He is an old shriveled man. He can barely walk."

"Let him come in," said the queen graciously.

The girl went back outside and picked up her broom. "You may enter. There will be food and drink at nightfall."

"Thank you, maiden." The corpselike specter entered the hall.

Within he saw the glittering carvings of deer, wolves, ravens. Although the light was low, even the dregs of sunlight made the gilded walls shine. Older girls soon came out to light the oil lamps and the flames shot out like rays of sunbeams to illuminate the gilded hall. He drew in his breath at the light within the hall, a haven of warmth on the black and wind-whipped heath. "Isn't it beautiful?" asked the girl, hearing his sudden intake. "It's the firelight in the midst of winter. Here all is good and peaceful."

She did not see the ancient one smile grimly.

The girl led the stranger to a bench far from the giftstool. Some warriors were already drinking and laughed to see such a corpse sit among them.

"Care to fight with us, stranger?" taunted one youth over his golden brew.

"Leave him alone," said the girl sharply.

"Is he your grandfather, girl?" retorted the warrior.

"No. He is a guest. And like all guests he must be treated with respect." She carried some food to the old man who dug in eagerly, nervously eyeing the rough warriors who were gathering in number.

Other young women entered bearing cups of liquid gold and platters high with steaming victuals. The king and queen sat before their people and laughed at the rough humor of the warriors. The old man hung back, silent in fear.

The girl periodically checked on him to make sure he was not bothered and that he was taken care of. She was a good princess.

Finally the king beckoned the stranger to rise and join him. "Tell us, stranger, from where do you come? How did you find our hall? What news of the outside world can you share?"

The old man, still hunched, his grey cloak covering his head, answered in a shaky voice. "I am a wanderer. My lord died many seasons ago. He had protected and loved me. Then he was killed. Now I wander the seas and roads seeking out a new lord to tether to."

"Why have you found none, pitiful soul?" asked the king.

"None has thought me worthy. I am old and near death. No leader wants a weak corpse as his soldier. Though I would fight to defend such a leader to the death."

The warriors laughed.

"You would be knocked down when we rushed by, ancient one!" one shouted. "A fine lot of good that would do a lord."

The king interrupted. "Such a man has nothing to lose—not family, name, or youth. He would defend a worthy lord. Many a loud talker in the meadhall would turn tail from the onslaught of enemies if his precious life were threatened. An old grey wolf would stay to the end."

The young warriors fell silent.

"Here," said the king, gesturing that the old man should approach the giftstool, "take this clasp." The king handed the greybeard an inlaid piece of finely wrought jewelry. The old man looked at it carefully.

"It should belong to a younger man, not one such as I," he protested at last.

"And so it once did," said the king after a long pause. "He is gone forever from these halls and is not likely to return. Here, you, o faithful friend, may have this as a tribute of faith and friendship."

A smile could be made out in the folds of his grey cloak. "I thank you, lord," quavered the voice.

"I am Hrothgar, lord of the Scyldings, king of the Danes. Many fear me. My followers across the seas are well rewarded. As shall your faithful service be."

The grey cloaked one bowed, grasping the clasp with his withered hand. He walked back to his seat.

"Let us drink to our circle of peace," said the queen in her deep and musical voice. She stepped forward bearing high a golden cup, studded with blood red and grass green jewels sparkling in the lamplight. Her husband drank, then each warrior and maiden, counselor and wife. The lady wove a web of peace in passing the chalice.

The singing scop stepped forth and told of heroes and dragons, ships and storms, maidens and marriage. The lamplights flickered, fountains of oil. The women returned to their quarters, the king joined the queen. He stopped by to wish the old man a good sleep. "Here," said the king handing him a wolf pelt, "sleep warm. Old bones get cold in a darkened hall." The sovereign moved on as the aged retainer bowed his head. He lay down on the thick rug, pulling it around him for warmth. He heard belches, farts, and laughter from the doughty fighters, who soon fell asleep.

After some time, all that could be heard were snores, some loud and whistling, some calm and gentle breaths. The old man stirred beneath his thick rug. Drawing back his rough cloak, he looked about. Not a warrior was roused. He stood up, first couching, then fully erect. Miraculously, he no longer hunched over. His shriveled form seemed magically to broaden. He grew tall, seeming as strong as those boasters of the golden hall. Over his massive shoulders he had thrown the wolf pelt. From beneath his tattered, ragged cloak, he drew forth a gleaming object. Slowly and silently, he walked in the shadows of the darkened room. He approached the giftstool. On the seat of the throne he placed something.

Then to the nearest warrior he went. Over he bent. A grunt could be heard. After a moment, he stood up again. Gently he covered up the warrior with his fur wrap. Holding a heavy weight beneath his grey ragged cloth, he slid through the inky shadows of the hall. His bright eyes took in the scene—a sleepy, peaceful pool of rest, undisturbed by any ripple of trouble. If you had looked carefully through the murk at his face, you would have seen a grim smile stretch his lips briefly. Opening the door of the hall, he slipped out into the black of night. He covered the heath along the path to the sea as swiftly as a stalking wolf. His shadow melted into the night.

In the morning, the warriors mumbled and groaned awake. Light filtered in through the smoke hole of the roof. The smells of freshly baked bread wafted into the hall. Gradually they stood up, singly and in groups going outdoors to piss, their penises shriveling in the chill wind of winter.

One fighter slept on, curled up near the king's throne. "Get up, you lazy sot," cried one playful trooper, kicking—none too gently—the somnolent figure. The sleeping warrior stretched out at the blow and his fellows laughed. The merriment suddenly stopped when they saw their comrade's body fall back—without his head. Their mouths, wreathed by hair, opened in surprise, disbelief, and horror.

The girl walked in to announce the coming morning repast when she saw their dumb looks. "Shall I throw the bread into your gaping maws?" she joked and then looked to where their gaze was frozen. She saw the severed neck, wet with black gore.

"Get her out," cried one warrior who had his wits about him. "Tell your father to come at once!"

She left, happy to obey since her understanding had not yet caught up with her senses.

"Father! Father!" she shrieked, rushing to his chamber, the only fully private one in the women's quarters. She rushed in, oblivious to her father's grey-haired chest and her mother's body, naked beneath a fur blanket.

"What is it, Freawaru?" shouted her father angrily, sitting up.

She could not speak. She pointed. No sounds could come from her throat, only strange cries like those of a slaughtered lamb. "The hall," she managed to utter at last, " —blood — "

Hrothgar pulled on his cloak, Wealhtheow close behind him. The queen held Freawaru back, saying, "Stay with me, my dear. This is man's business."

Surely, thought Freawaru, this is woman's business, too. We are the ones married off as peaceweaving brides after the blood and gore have barely dried.

Hrothgar turned the body over. He sighed, then stood up. "Where is the stranger from last night?"

"Gone," one answered.

Hrothgar saw the clasp. It had once belonged to his oldest son, now exiled from the hall, the clasp he gifted the old wanderer the eve before.

"Shall we follow him, your lordship? We can trace the drops of blood. We can catch up with him and— " Here the warrior made a frightening sound.

Hrothgar looked at the clasp he held in his hand. "No," he said slowly. "It is no use. I know where he is. This is a message.

Only I can respond."

Hrothgar sat on the giftstool.

"Your lordship, we must act now. If you know where this man is, tell us where so we can avenge this murderous act."

Hrothgar stared out into the shadows of the hall, faintly gleaming in the grey of morning.

Æschere, trusted counselor, spoke. "He lives by the snake-infested mere, across a bog no mortal man can pass. He is the moorwalker, the gloom-goer. No human warrior can match him. He is a shape-changer. His mother's magic protects him from detection. He can come and go here as he pleases, as an old man, perhaps next time as a luscious young woman. It is best to let fate decide."

Unferth burst out, "He will come again and again and again, until the giftstool is his."

One cocky young warrior boldly said, "Her magic is not so strong."

Æschere sighed. "Even if we kill him, he can never be defeated." The older warrior knew whereof he spoke. "Besides, the people still love Grendel and his mother. If we killed them, there would be revenge. We are threatened no matter what we do."

Wealhtheow and Freawaru came into the hall.

"Her powers covered my eyes from the horrible truth until too late." Hrothgar sighed. "I know he will come after me. He does not wish to kill me, only to drive me to a death without honor. How can I avenge a spirit of the night?"

A memory sparked in young Freawaru, told of the night wanderer. Hadn't there been such a one not many years since who had once protected her from the taunts of the warriors? Could that strapping youth have shriveled into the grey wretch of last night?

"Come with me, Freawaru," commanded her mother. The girl returned to the women's quarters. She would not forget the blood sprinkled on the hall floor, nor the genuine gratitude of the old man she had helped. How could both be true?

The young man did not bother to hurry. Hrothgar knew where he could find him. Grendel smiled. It had all gone so smoothly. He hated to abuse young Freawaru's goodness like that. It couldn't be helped. The object he carried grew heavy as he walked, the sticky warm goo soaking his cloak.

He smiled in the grey of dawn, making his way over the sickly bright green bog on the tufts he knew were safe to step on. The hovel by the mere was his realm, though not his alone.

"Mother!" he called out, when he came in. "Mother," he said more quietly. She sat by the fire, stirring some brew in the black cauldron.

She arose, a smile breaking through her drawn cheeks. She opened her arms. "Grendel!" she cried with joy. Then he held up his prize, its eyes dull, the face drained and white. Slowly her arms dropped. "What have you done?" she gasped, knowing full well the truth.

"I am the heir to the throne. He cannot drive you and me away," said Grendel matter-of-factly, placing the head by the hearth. "Trophies like these will lead us to our rightful place again."

She shook her head. "No, my love, we can never return to the hall. Not in triumph." She looked around the hovel sheltering them. "This is our hall now, and you the lord and I the lady of it. He will not harm us here if we sit quiet. For you to kill his most beloved followers, that way lies madness."

"Does it, Mother?" Grendel smiled. "I don't feel mad. In fact, for the first time in years I feel calm. I feel at peace."

"That frightens me. I wish this" —she pointed to the head— "would torment you. We can't destroy Hrothgar. I know that all too well. He is too powerful."

"He isn't Odin, Mother. He's no god. Just the brutal terrorizer of squalid little villages. There's nothing noble in that."

"I never said he was noble. He is stronger than we are. I told you when this all started we should leave his land, abandon the past and create a new future for us. You insisted on staying here. Why? Why? You are young, Grendel. You have promise. Elsewhere you could find a truly worthy lord to follow."

"To follow? To follow? I—follow? I am a leader. I am the king's son. I desire to rule the hall when he dies. And so I shall."

"Revenge will destroy you."

"Revenge will save me. I haven't been this happy in years."

His mother looked at the head. She wrinkled her nose in distaste. "I never did like that man. Take out the garbage, won't you, my dear?"

Grendel smiled. He picked up the head and walked outside. He threw it into the burbling muck and watched it sink slowly into the goo. Then he came back in. His mother looked at him from head to foot. "I hate getting rid of bloodstains."

Grendel smiled. "You're a darling, Mother." He kissed her.

"And you're a naughty boy." She embraced him, then stood back. The blood had stained her cloak, too. "Now I am in it with you," she said.

"You have been from the start, Mother."

The start. His mother's origins were as murky as the shadows in the darkened, threatened meadhall.

Grendel knew that story. How many times had she told him her tale, the lay of a lady long ago. At night around the fire there was little to do but talk. Words burbled up from the black cauldron warming their soup, their sustenance for the hate and revenge they carried within, giving their lives meaning and hope.

Chapter 18

Embracing Death

Over the half-years, as winter followed winter, Brimhild simmered herbal lore and prophetic knowledge mastered only by crafty women. Brimhild drew on her keen memory to draw forth what Ælfsciene had taught her long since. A leechbook holding secrets of life shaped their sad subsistence on the desperate mere edge.

She bid Grendel carry vervain with him at all times, so he would not be barked at by dogs. Then he could slip into the hall unseen and unnoticed. Brimhild uttered the spells which the wise woman Gróa chanted after the hero Svipdag woke her from the grave. She spoke the loosening spell, to free his limbs and legs. She conjured the weather spell, to lull wild wind and water. She uttered the speech spell, to grant him wit and words. Svipdag would be successful so long as he followed Gróa's bidding. So, too, would Grendel thrive if he followed Brimhild's wisdom.

Season after season Grendel returned to Heorot, only to be challenged. His superior training made him a dangerous foe, though his intentions were pure. Many a man may die, when diplomacy is avoided.

To rid them of Grendel's mischief, the Danish lord had mandrake wort brought into the middle of the hall to expel all evils. At all times the king carried with him a twig of feltwort, so he would not feel any awe or terror at the coming evil. Hrothgar, hero of the Scyldings, stood for his tribe. Shamen boiled lupins, hedgerife, bishopwort, red maythe, cropleek, and salt in butter. They smeared the king with the salve, to cure the country of nocturnal goblin visitors.

Sacrifice was no stranger to the glory-hall. Hrothgar called on the priests of spirit lore. Beasts were killed.

When the soul-slayer remained silent, they remembered older ways. The shaman spoke to Inga. The virgin agreed, voiced her assent.

When Hrothulf, Hrothgar's nephew, his foster-son, saw her, he felt desire, alive. "Why do you consent? You need not! I will take you now so you will be no virgin. They cannot sacrifice you then."

Inga could not explain her conviction that this was to be her end. "My sister and I were twinned at the death of our mother at Scylding hands. I have loved you on time borrowed from fate. You can rape me and deny me my moment of sacrament. I will not prize you for it. Let me create a life which signifies."

He became heavy at heart. No words or battle could stop the bloody oblation. He embraced her body at last, slumped with slaughter.

For this, Hrothulf nursed grief in his breast.

Dead flesh, so cold,
last night I held you to my breast.
I felt your heart beat against mine.
The ember's glow glinted
off your red-gold hair.
I smelled your skin.

But now
you are hard and pale.
My fingers cannot stroke you,
warm and quivering.
O dead one,
you have betrayed me.
How dare you leave me here
alone and alive?
Why didn't you kill me

when you chose your fate?

I hate you, Beloved,
for letting me lose myself
in my love for you.
My flesh is warm
my heart cannot still.
I turn hard and pale.

My next embrace
will be of death.

Chapter 19

How Can You Love Me?

Once, after twenty seasons, when Grendel, son of sadness, returned to the hate-hall, he heard a soft voice whisper to him beside the road to Heorot, a stony path he skirted along. Grendel froze. His breath stopped.

"Grendel? It is I, Freawaru, your sister."

"Half-sister," he angrily replied. "What do you want?"

"I have watched you secretly. I know you come when the moon is dark. I have seen you glide, an alone-walker on the moor."

"Whom have you told?" he demanded, grasping his sword.

"No one," she cried. "I remember, when I was a child, my cousin Hrothulf teased me. He mocked my hair and said it looked like rope. You had no love for me, yet you told him such a rope may save a foamy-necked ship at sea. For that I have always been grateful to you. I would not betray you."

Grendel loosened his grip on the sword. "How old are you now?"

"Thirty-four half-years. I still hate Hrothulf. He glowers so."

"What can you tell of the hall?"

"My father thinks only of you, Grendel. I know who you are and what happened. I think it's unfair."

"Who told you?"

"Don't be angry. I overheard Unferth."

"That fool!"

"A powerful one."

Grendel made no reply.

"What do they say about me?"

"Do you really want to know?"

"Would I ask otherwise?" he growled.

"They say you are no son of my father. They say a priest slept with your mother. They say you killed thanes, to whom you'd sworn brotherhood. Spilled blood must be avenged."

Grendel was in a fury. "Hrothgar is my father!"

"I believe you. I know what is a lie and what is truth."

"Do you, Freawaru? You are only a girl."

"I am a princess," she responded hotly. "I may be young. Yet I can feel lies that burn my ears."

Grendel did not respond. Then Freawaru spoke, more gently now.

"Do you remember the earth-sanctuary we hid in as children?"

"Yes. Though my childhood seems to belong to another man."

"Meet me there, Grendel. I want to help you."

"Perhaps. When?"

"The next dark of the moon."

Grendel hesitated. He yearned to know of his father, far-off friend, fell foe. "I will come."

Then he reached for her, touched her shoulder. She ran off.

Weeks passed and Grendel made his way to the old sanctuary, a grave barrow. Dozens of them littered the landscape, great lumps in the heath. This one sat between the hall and the shore. It had been built generations ago for the ancient rites of Grendel's ancestors. The barrow had once served as an artificial cave for the harried Danes to escape notice from marauding tribes. Huge boulders formed the walls. The children played there, terrified of the spirits of the dead, though bones no longer decorated the earth. They had once been used as toy weapons by boys now long dead.

The stone threshold had a rotting wooden door. Grendel suspected a plot. He feared being trapped.

And he was. Though not as he had expected.

Stooping, he entered the earthhole, holding out his sword. He heard a noise. "Who's there?" he asked, wielding his metal friend.

"Me, Grendel. Don't fear."

An oil lamp was lighted. And there was the trap set for him—the face of a woman, her hair a malice net, golden fetters for his heart.

He could not speak.

She could.

Your hand on my shoulder
scared me.
I fled like a deer hunted by Actaeon.
Or, perhaps,
you're the stag
Actaeon became,
torn apart by
your own desires,
tearing apart mine.

Later that night he laughed.

Grendel found he could not wait for another month to pass. And another. He spoke:

I worship Artemis,
goddess of the moon,
for without the moon
my lover and I
could never meet.

We touch beneath
its silver rays
in secret groves
protected by our deity,
the fearsome huntress.

We track one another,
hunter and hunted,
we cannot tell
who stalks whom
in our chaste pursuit.

Still, I fear the fate of Actaeon,
made vulnerable,
bewitched by love,
taken by desire,
on glimpsing the lunary protectress.

Transformed,
he was torn apart
by his own loyal hounds.
Will I, likewise,
be destroyed by my own
riveting desires?

After slaughtering a hoary retainer, he came to her covered with hot blood. She could not resist him, angry avenger. The slender maid lay in his arms, seduced by love. He found himself trapped, beguiled like Sigmund by his sister Signy. Njorth, too, knew his sister; their children were Freyr and Freya.

Incredulous, Grendel questioned Freawaru.

I almost killed that little moth
intruding on our heart to heart.
You stopped me, protesting its innocence,
and I felt ashamed.
If you can love that little moth
I almost killed so thoughtlessly,
how can you love me?

She replied.

We are held together
by numberless burdens.
If they all disappeared,
we too might fly out
into the heavens
and speed away
further and further
from one another
until I'd appear to you
as only a small, receding light.

Grendel soon forgot to glide under cover of darkness. He sought out the light and met the white-armed woman by the moon's sickle sheen. Before a month seemed short. Now a night of pining crept by, endless longing. Heartsick, he yearned when not in her chains.

His mother's loosening spell had not counted on shackles so soft and pale.

He thought of his woman.

She stands
between sky and earth,
rooted in the solid ground
that cannot betray her step.
The loam is firm and stable.

She — burrowed in soil,
attuned to heaven —
carries more substance
than I —
just a dream,
a trick of the light

you see out of the corner of your eye.

Freawaru would beg Grendel to plead for mercy. "I cannot be happy unless we can be wed. I want to be with you always."

"We will be together until death," promised Grendel. "Though that day may be near."

"Must you be so gloomy?"

"I'm not gloomy!" he protested. "I'm joyful. I've found you." He kissed her cheeks, licked the tears away. "I was gloomy when I wasn't an outlaw."

Freawaru laughed at this grim joke. "How can you be so sarcastic? Your father has rejected you, there is a blood price on your head, your mother is in exile, too. How can this be better than before?"

"Before I had to act as my father wished. When I didn't, he despised me. The shame I felt from his aversion to me was far worse than being on the run. As an outcast, I need only please myself. I can fashion myself to be whom I choose."

"A hated foe?"

"A passionate lover, a skillful killer, and loyal son."

Freawaru could not accept this perverse acceptance of his wrongful banishment. He was innocent. Her father was not. Grendel seemed to revel in what he saw as freedom, what she deeply sensed to be captivity by oppressive kin.

She rebuked him. "You may feel free out on your stinking mere. I have to return every dawn to that hall of hatred. I have to listen to their plots against you. I have to help them plan and scheme for your death."

"And so you tell me what is intended and I can avoid the trap," pointed out Grendel.

"I must live as two beings!" she cried out. "I cannot be split like this. I hate my father, for you. I love him, for me. You are now me and so I am twinned, battling against my own self."

"Flee with me!" urged Grendel, not for the first time. "Come live with us on the mere. My mother would welcome you."

"No hall should have more than one peaceweaver, Grendel. Surely you learned that when my mother came to Heorot. I know your mother is aware of the strife caused by two queens," Freawaru added drily.

"We have no hall. It is a hovel."

"All the more reason for me to stay away. She'd feel shame no doubt, before her rival's daughter."

"Before her son's beloved? Never!"

"Grendel, what shall we do?" asked Freawaru simply.

"Let us go abroad." Grendel caressed her body, willing it to flee with him.

"And leave your mother?"

"Take her with us. We can start anew."

"As refugees, fugitives, exiles?" Freawaru was too deeply bound to abandon her place.

Peaceweaving flowed in her veins. Such a woman will stay until the last warrior falls into a pool of his own blood. Then she will be led off, captive.

Grendel knew, much as it tormented her, she would never leave the hall. And so, he himself would never leave.

Four seasons passed.

What if we hid in the woods,
cutting bracken,
trampling undergrowth,
forging fresh footpaths?

In the virgin thicket,
will our lovework seal
or open new vistas?
Perhaps both/and.

Chapter 20

The Youth's Journey

The bearded man stood above a seated youth, who sulked into his mead cup. The king, massive and broad, was actually no taller than the younger man who had yet to fill out his chest with bands of muscles won in combat. The elder of the two was dressed in a dark purple robe in the Roman style, delicate golden clasps at his shoulder. He chose his words carefully and could not disguise the concern and anger in his voice.

"When you were only a boy, no one minded this behavior. It's understandable. In fact, it bodes well for one's manhood when a boy has high spirits with his bedfellow. After the first spring or autumn trip, however, that behavior is no longer tolerated. That initial journey is meant to make a man of you. You know how we have perfected the manner in which we subdue a native population. Through the women."

"Against their will," spat out the youth, half in remembered pleasure, half in disgust.

"How else to gain their compliance? Or that of their men? Those few men who fight get killed. The rest—with their wives and children—we sell. And we have profited greatly that way. Oh, every so often a man may take a genuine fancy to the woman he has—" Here the king shrugged his shoulders and smiled. "She may join our happy band. Most of them are like pieces of silver or gold—a means of trade." The man paused. "You had your first trip over two years ago."

"I did my—" and here the youth sneered, revealing his teeth, "—duty."

"Indeed. Now your duty remains to be done here. Forget your childish affections. He is to be your comrade-at-arms. With him you will violate many women. There can no longer be—" again,

147

an awkward pause, distaste in his voice, "—that sort of thing between you. And anyway," said the king, turning suddenly from the youth, "there's many a luscious young thing here who would be happy to, shall we say, entertain you."

"Who?" the youth asked.

"Hygd, for one."

"What makes you think she like me?"

Hygelac laughed. "So, you're interested? She told her nursemaid she thought you'd make a fine man if you left off fondling your cradle companion."

Beowulf blushed. "She's not even twelve summers old."

"She will be soon. If you don't snap her up, I may. As my consort."

Beowulf was aghast. "You can't mean it."

"Why not?" asked the king. "I'm not decrepit. And women love power."

"Well," stumbled out Beowulf, "even if I wanted to sleep with her, I couldn't. Such girls aren't to be touched before they marry."

"There are other girls," and Hygelac winked, looking in the direction of the kitchens and slave quarters, "who need not be so careful."

Beowulf still glowered down into his cup. He drank a few sips. He needed to keep his wits about himself when near the king, his foster-uncle.

"Look, boy," said Hygelac, now sitting down and putting his arm around his nephew's shoulder, "it is thought that you had better go away for a few seasons."

"What?" Beowulf was amazed. "To do what?"

"To become a man. Our spring and autumn trips have not helped you to get over your old ways. You have lots of energy. Expend it as many a young man does—through travel. Go off and make a name for yourself. When you return, you may have outgrown your boyish—fancies?—and become worthy of your fate. Besides, Hygd will be a woman, then."

"If she hasn't been wed."

Hygelac laughed. "I'm not trying to get rid of you. It has been suggested to me most vehemently in counsel that I have been altogether too lax with you due to our family tie. No other youth would have been allowed such a long period of dissipation. See things my way. I've been too soft with you. It's weakened my position. Surely you don't want me to lose my grip on the gift-stool."

"Of course not, Uncle," said the boy-man.

"Then do me a favor. Take off as they request. I'll fit you out with a splendid longship, supplies, and men."

Beowulf looked up, hooding his eyes. "May Hondscio come with me?"

Hygelac thought for a moment. "He needs to grow up too. I want you to promise that you two will desist from—" He didn't finish.

"I will try, Uncle." Beowulf sounded none too happy.

"And go see Hygd before you go. She would love to talk with you, I imagine."

Preparations took several weeks. They could not depart until the salty sound began to thaw. The morning they embarked, Beowulf visited with Hygd. A child still, the amber-haired poppet came to him, carrying green garlands.

"Beowulf, I heard you were to leave this day. I brought you this mistletoe for good luck."

He looked down at the green petals and white berries. "How is it good luck? Baldr was killed with mistletoe. His mother had neglected to extract a promise from that plant alone not to harm her son. Then Loki, that tricky god, arranged for Baldr's end."

"I know," agreed Hygd. "I asked this mistletoe not to harm you. And to bid all her fellow plants to refrain from injuring you. I think the gods will respect my petition."

Beowulf accepted the greenery. "I hope they do. Only the gods can render our fate. A pretty girl's request can't harm their help."

Hygd's cheeks flooded with pink.

"When I return, Hygd, you'll be a woman. Will you wait for me?" He almost loved her. He liked to see her blush.

The girl took all words as true and straight. "I'll wait if there's a reason to wait." She looked him coolly in the eyes, like a practiced temptress. Perhaps all girls are born with the ability to challenge men.

"I may fall in love with a Slavic princess."

"Perhaps you won't be able to forget your companion. You're always hand-in-glove with him," she sharply teased.

Beowulf angered. "Do what you wish, maiden. When I am a man, you will regret those words."

And she would.

Hygd stamped her delicate foot and spun away in a flounce. Beowulf threw back his head and roared with laughter. Hondscio came up. "What's so funny?"

Beowulf looked after the girl, still hurrying away. "Now I see why men sleep with women. For the pleasure of tormenting them."

As Beowulf's longship sailed out of the small fiord harbor protecting Hygelac's fleet, an icy wind roared down from the north filling its sails. That wind raced across the sound, over that single ship destined to wander the eastern seas for many seasons, until it hit the ice floes and islands further south. It screamed down one long fiord, quieting as it went. Reaching land, it blew icicle breath. Up the heathland it came, blocked on its path by the glorious hall, imposing and secure.

Chapter 21

Blood Eagle

The group of warriors arrived from Sweden. Their leader had been feckless and wanton in his youth. The Storm-Geats told him to improve himself abroad. He and his rowdy companions set off on a trail of destruction around the Baltic Sea. One day they arrived in the land of the Spear-Danes. Beowulf, warrior of the Weders, owed a favor to Hrothgar. The Scylding king had once helped Beowulf's father, Ecgtheow. Now was the time for the son to make his own fame. He had heard of a murderous marauder picking off retainers at random in the glory-hall called Heorot and vowed to finish off the fiend.

Beowulf, son of Ecgtheow, sat on the mead-benches of the humbled hall.

"Your father I once knew, Beowulf," declaimed Hrothgar. "He killed Heatholaf of the Wylfings. The treaty-folk sent him here. I paid his wergild and took Wealhtheow as my reward."

"I have come to pay back my father's debt."

"I have heard that Breca the Bronding outswam you among sea-monsters," taunted Unferth.

"Who are you? Brother to Loki, trickster of poison words?"

"I am Unferth, son of Ecglaf."

"Ah, the brother killer. Of you I have heard tell. So, too, the sons of Gudrun, Sorli and Hamthir, killed their brother Erp. They missed him sorely after hewing Jormunrek's limbs."

"Fratricide is no stranger to your family, son of Ecgtheow. You are nephew to Hæthcyn, who killed your uncle Herebeald."

"That was an accident."

"Accident or no, I heard that Hrethel, their father, died of grief. I have also heard tell that the Geats worship Freya like women, posing like wives. Are you not a member of the nation

151

where woman rules? Such is a sign of decline below freedom, worse than decent slavery."

"Those are the Finns. Besides, Odin and Loki acted like women, it is said, weaving spells, birthing the eight-legged horse, growing large with ogres. No one questions their manhood. At least I fight when there is a battle. I don't hide in the outbuildings while terror ensues, kissing women for fear of the victory-twig."

"Glory I don't need to seek out abroad."

"A deep drinker dims his reason."

"When my tongue lashes out, you protect your pride."

"Much mead muddies thought."

"Such strong words show how mighty you warriors may be," interrupted Hrothulf. "Odin once advised never to mock a wayfaring guest. You know not who he may be. Better cause strife to the intruder, the berserker and shape-changer, Grendel by name."

They feasted and drank. All save Beowulf. He kept his head clear, ascetic assassin. Several days passed, pausing by mead benches. Beowulf sensed a shadow slide, disappear onto the moor. He followed the maiden's steps, waited in darkness, his breath turned to fog. Nightly he made this pilgrimage, planning his offering to an altar of blood.

Freawaru told Grendel of Beowulf's coming, hopeful of ruling the battlefield. Her beloved brother laughed to think of Beowulf's foolishness, Geatish yokel. "Perhaps my sword will sweat with his blood, that of the Geatish goon." The sibling lovers mingled their loins and slept.

Then they heard men's hard feet, stomping the frozen ground. Grendel sat up, grasped his sword, reached for his spell-hardened shield. Freawaru covered herself with her cloak, shielding her bared breasts, gleaming in candlelight.

Beowulf entered with a dozen men. They gathered around Grendel.

"No!" screamed Freawaru.

I have been told men held that struggling youth. Then sword gave good service, piercing the belly. Beowulf severed ribs, pulled out lungs. He cut the blood-eagled bird of gore. He was no stranger to carving. Grendel was covered in dew of sorrow. Beowulf kicked the corpse savagely. Freawaru screamed and raved. She had no chance for one last talk with him, hewn for hawks, ravaged for ravens. Broken by foemen, her bosom friend was dead.

The men surrounded her.

The whalebone casket
depicts the vengeance of Weland,
smith of the gods,
fashioning fetters never falling away
and swords of uncommon strength.
He made beauty out of bone:
the boy's skull a jewelled goblet,
guzzled from by the unknowing father,
drinking liquor from scooped out bonehouse.
After raping Baduhild,
Weland flew off on magic wings.

The smith makes art from death.
Even he could not make
the sea become bone.
Yet, this wonder I once saw.

Later they brought Grendel's head to Heorot. Mead joy rang in the hall. Hrothgar heard the noise, happy hubbub. He left his wife's side, lovely lady, for the hero's news.

"He's dead, my king," said Beowulf proudly, holding the head up for Hrothgar to see.

Hrothgar smiled grimly to see his boy, the child of love, the grandchild of lust and violence, cut and bloodied, dirty with death.

No creature wept. Brimhild did not yet know of her son's demise.

"This blood cleanses Heorot," said Hrothgar. "Let us rejoice."

I have heard that Hrothgar received no featherless hawk, as Randver had sent his father, King Jonakr. That ruler had hung his own son on the gallows. He was no Abraham, sacrificing at God's behest. That king was jealous of Randver on account of the beautiful Svanhild. Bold Bikki, cruel counselor, gave ill advice, salacious slander. Jonakr agreed to kill his son, clan killing. Later the king drove horses at Svanhild, heavy hooves weighing her down into the dust. That hairless bird, sent after the son's slaughter, meant no honor for King Jonakr. Like a crippled fowl, the father had ruined his kingdom.

They took Grendel's body to the tree by the mere. The headless corpse rode on the gallows, woeful wolftree. Likewise, Odin hung from the World Tree. Spear-stabbed, he won rune secrets. Grendel only gained of his true parentage, deadly descent.

Chapter 22

The Angel of Death

That night Brimhild dreamt of a great horse, portending a death by hanging. Later, hidden in hovel, the mother was visited by Freawaru, maddened maid.

The lover and the mother mourned Grendel's death, feared for his fame.

They suffered more than Gjaflaug, Herborg, and Gullrond, those widowed ladies each claiming she was most unhappy. When Sigurd died, Gudrun sat over his dead corpse. Then she was the most woeful wife. Yet Brimhild and Freawara defeated that woman's dejection, darkened that despair.

Taletellers bragged how Beowulf killed Grendel barehanded. The death was gleefully gloried as a well-deserved slaughter, the butchery of unclean meat. Freawaru told of the bleeding offering, ritual death. Tears pricked at Brimhild's eyelids, like the dampness of a thaw setting in after frost. Duty controlled her. Her only love now destroyed, she seethed for revenge to gladden the raven.

To help her fight against her foe, she boiled swallow nestlings in wine, then ate them before she went. Dressing herself in cloth woven from thin and wretched goats, Brimhild travelled, hooded, towards Heorot. A knife she tucked at her waist, along with a bag woven of dragon fell. She ducked around corners and lurked in doorways in the pearly mist of twilight.

Heorot hummed with mirth.

Brimhild waited until the cries of drunken buffoonery ended and the scop's voice quieted. The hall was still and dim. She crept within. Knowing every beam in her hall, she slid in the shadows. The light glowed brightly by Hrothgar's throne and hers, now usurped by an alien womb. There hung was the dripping severed head of her golden boy, eyes shut to horror and wonder. She cradled his crown, consigned it to fire-snake skin. Making out lumps of warriors sleeping, some snoring in peaceful oblivion, she chose the retainer closest to Hrothgar's chair, the beloved Æschere. Quiet and quick, her knife flashed in the drear dim. She made a caesura between head and body and carried her prize warm and dripping beneath her cloak, a Judith who conquered Holofernes. She felt glee in her grim revenge.

In the morning, the throbbing heads of the warriors slowed their senses. Adjusting their eyes to the early light, they noticed one warrior succumbed to the night joys. They playfully teased him, all wound up and snoozing, dead to the world. "Æschere, you lazy sot! Get up and kiss the ladies who greet you!" Beowulf came over and shouted, "You sodden fool! It's time to awaken!" and kicked him. Over fell Æschere, burly and strong, with nothing amiss but his head.

The ladies fainted and men grew pale. They saw that the trophy was absent. A trail of blood led to the door. The men armed themselves quickly.

"It's her!" whispered Hrothgar. "She wants to destroy me!"

"Now we will hurt the Angel of Death!" proclaimed Beowulf over beer.

"Who is that creature?" asked Hrothgar.

Beowulf spoke, told his tale. "Once, when I travelled far to the east, to the great river swollen with ice, I witnessed the Angel of Death. A dead chief was accompanied to his beyond with a female slave who volunteers her life. Before her end, she drinks to celebrate her coming triumph. She lies with the master of each household, each one saying unto her: 'Tell your master I do this thing for the love of him.'

"She drinks a potion and proclaims, 'I see my father and mother! I see my dead relatives! I see my master in Paradise, calling me! Let me go to him!'

"The Angel of Death, a huge woman, stern and severe, takes

the wench to the tent on a ship. Men beat their shields to cover her cries. Six men enter the tent and lie with her. She is placed by her dead master. The men strangle her with a noose while the Angel of Death stabs her again and again and again between the ribs.

"Then those living escape the ship while it is consumed in flames.

"The slave girl is like Heorot. Your kingdom, Hrothgar, is penetrated and slain by Grendel. Now he is dead and his mother, the Angel of Death, has been mortally touched. Death, thou willt die. We will trap her with honey, like the she-wolf when Signy smeared Sigmund's face and tongue. Siggeir's mother, wolf woman, reached her tongue into the warrior's mouth and he bit it off. That was her death. So Signy killed her mother-in-law, treacherous troll."

Beowulf continued, consoling the king. "I dreamt of a snake pursuing me, Lord of the Victory-Scyldings. That signifies that I should be on my guard against an evil woman. I'll get her, my king. I've always fulfilled my intentions where slaughter is concerned."

"It is best not to stop with a witch, even though nightfall is near. Beware of her spells or you'll lie in her bed, never to wake a free man."

Beowulf went with all of his warriors, fierce fighters following the bloody path to the fen. They hurried across the moor to the edge of the stinking mere. Unferth went with them to show them the way, knowing of Brimhild's hovel betwixt land and sea. "She lives in a horror hall, neither on dirt nor water. She is a trickster and her son a monster!"

Eager for bloodsport, they hurried along until they arrived at the edge of the mere. Sea snakes swam in the fearful fen.

Unferth said, "If only we had such a one as Gunnar with us. King Atli wanted his treasure, Fafnir's lair. Gunnar was put in the serpent pit by Atli, his sister's husband. Though his hands were bound fast, he played the harp with his toes. He sent the serpents to sleep, all save one, aggressive adder. Gunnar could lull these lizards to lethargy. His sister Gudrun would later avenge his death."

Strange water-fire lit the men's faces. Bright green patches marked tuffets of safety—or death? The heavily-laden warriors paused and reflected. Mute they saw resting peacefully and calm, on a verdant hillock over quicksand, the severed head of their comrade at arms, smiling in dreamless slumber. Unferth removed his sword, laid it carefully on tough turf. Making for the ghastly lump, Unferth's boots glued in the muck. "Help me!" he cried. They held out their hands, too far to assist. They watched then in horror as Unferth sank low, eels embracing him sweet and slow. The last gurgle of breath was heard, the final bubble of air popped. Their eyes glued on the death spring of the kin-killer.

Then they saw the maiden, Freawaru, bending over the bog, merciful mere. "Grendel, my Grendel, the trouble upon me wounds my mind." She held a knife, staining the sea with scarlet.

"Grab her!" shouted Beowulf. "Return her to court," he ordered his companion, who held her arms, gleaming with gore.

"I watched Unferth die! You wrangling warriors are bobbing for barbarians, fishing for foreigners." She laughed too long. Beowulf struck her, silencing her sounds.

Eyes devoid of dancing looked out at him. "You save women who desire oblivion and abandon those who wish to be saved."

Then Beowulf, man of the War-Geats, barked a laugh. "No woman will conquer us! I'll get the bitch and teach her a lesson. She'll beg for the mercy of death!"

Carefully, cleverly, with wit of a bold idiot killer, Beowulf tested the hillocks of the mere. He brought with him Hruting, Unferth's blade. That sword might prove good luck. It would be bathed in blood. Beowulf made his way cunningly to the hovel hidden from his fellow killers behind the reeds.

Beowulf paused outside the hut. "Mere-wife!" he cried. "I

have come to avenge Æschere."

"Hrothgar should avenge his own son's death," he heard in reply.

"You speak in riddles, she-wolf."

"I am a riddle to foolish men."

"Await destruction."

"I have for many years. You need wait no longer for yours."

Beowulf entered her home. He was determined to punish her in the way he knew best when man attacks woman. She stood in the corner of her home, surrounded by herbs and medicinals, cups and bowls of concoctions. She controlled nature by wielding words and worts.

In a corner, Beowulf made out two eyes. He gasped, then realized they belonged to Grendel. His headless corpse lay there too. Brimhild had gathered his body parts. "Don't you wish to be welcomed as my hall-guest? Please sit," she graciously offered.

"This is no pleasant place," he said, indicating the smelly wormmeat.

"Grendel shall watch my end or my triumph. At least he shall know I died for his honor." She held out a cup. "A home is best, though it be small. I'd rather be mistress to my hovel and goats than to beg in a golden mead mansion. Though this is no radiant hall like Heorot, I wish to greet you as a woman of such a home should."

Beowulf drank, eyeing her carefully, searching out weapons or traps. She was no witless woman. "Why do you live in this hellhole?"

"My home was torn from me, my son murdered by you. I have nothing now. If I die, none will mourn. That poor girl," she gestured out the door to where the pitiful Freawaru had been dragged away, "will not think on me. I pray she remembers nothing." Then she looked at Beowulf. "I am not strong like you. Yet I can fight. I had my revenge through Æschere."

"He had nothing to do with your son's death, that coward. An appeaser, he spoke ever of saving you. Now he is dead. So must all weak men end. Now, welcome me, warrior-woman." Saying these words, Beowulf grabbed her roughly on her upper arms. He ripped her dress, exposing her white breasts where once the golden prince had suckled. He threw her to the floor and lifted her skirt. "This is how a Swede conquers a sea-bitch."

"And this is how a mere-wife exacts her revenge." She pointed to the half-empty cup he held. "That sweet nectar holds my monthly blood. You are powerless against it!" she cried. She grabbed the ceremonial cup, weaving revenge, throwing the contents over Beowulf's head. It dropped onto Hrunting, wanton weapon.

I have heard how he shrieked as the drink dripped down his shoulders and chest, incarnadine ink. Bereft of his manly prowess, Beowulf's weapon, boneless blade, melted. He felt his powers recede. To tame his virility, Brimhild had boiled water agrimony in Welsh ale. She approached him, battle-wife, monster-mother.

"Never shall you touch woman again."

This was not the curse of Gunnhild, who crippled Hrut in bed with his wife. Beowulf was to be no woman's husband. Later, Beowulf would wed no peace bride, have no heir. The Scylfings would come, Eadgils would avenge his brother's death and seek Wiglaf, son of Eanmund's killer, sweet savagery. Severe Swedes would plunder the pleasure palace, carry women and children into slavery.

Beowulf's kingdom was doomed to destruction.

He stepped out of the hut. Dusk had begun. He set foot into a watery soup, struggled to get out. "Help!" he called. "Help!" Beowulf was frantic, as his heavy armor dragged him deeper into the mere, wet weapon of woman.

Two of his men slowly approached, testing grassy stumps to see if they could bear their weight or were only false islands. So does the whale seem like an island to seafaring men. The sweet fragrance of that fish tricks travelers, doomed to drenching. They make secure the anchor on false land. Then the sly trickster plunges below, carrying wet warriors, drowned Danes, into the cavern of death.

One Weder, stalwart Swede, held out his arm. "Grasp me, my friend."

Hondscio, beloved blood brother, bent over Beowulf, whose weight dragged that companion in head first. The bubbles of Hondscio's last breath popped on the surface, his body sank down in a sweet swim of eternal sleep. That was Beowulf's bosom friend, his closest comrade. He fit Beowulf like a glove. Beowulf had no time to grieve a lover's lament.

"I'm almost there, Beowulf," said Froforgar, holding out a stick. "Hold on." After much effort, Beowulf extracted himself from the grim goo, the sickening slime. Covered in muck, he shuddered. Once they had pulled him from the ooze, he was besieged with questions. "Is she dead?" asked Froforgar.

"Yes," lied Beowulf. "Dead from this world of men and women. She has crossed over the borderland where frost giants and trolls reign." Froforgar took this to mean she had been killed.

So they told Hrothgar upon their return, lacking two warriors.

"She is dead? I am glad for it," said Hrothgar sincerely. "She must have been born on the fifth day of the moon, for that is when women die as witches and herbalists."

Beowulf told of his grievous journey, his war grief with the sea-wolf.

"The night-rider made me her hall-guest. That was no Glathsheim, or radiant hall, no Gimlé, or shining hall of the All-Father. It was not Vingólf, the sanctuary of goddesses. Hers is no Sessrúmnir with many seats as was Freya's homestead. Hers is built on Nástrandir, Corpse-Strands, poison drips from the lights in the roof, the building is woven from the backs of snakes. It was

Hel's realm of mist and darkness. Niflheim is her grave, dark dwelling of corpses and serpents, bitter cold, stench and rotting treasures.

"The corpse-greedy ogress gave me a potion. Grimhild gave one to Sigurd to forget cares, abandon Brynhild. Later, that witch's daughter, Gudrun, had her revenge. She hated King Atli, her second husband, killed their two sons. That was no love match. Atli drank from their skulls, goblets decorated with silver and gold. Mead he drank and the boys' blood, their hearts he consumed as well. She told him later what she had done and stabbed him to death. That was no happy man.

"Heith was a witch, wise seeress. Casting spells, she was always welcome to wicked women, like this berserk woman, she-wolf in her norn's nest. That crafty woman gave me bad brew, baleful blood.

"She made me fast with Gleipnir, magical fetter, made from the noise a cat makes when it moves, the beard of a woman, the roots of a mountain, the sinews of a bear, the breath of a fish, and the spittle of a bird. Fenrir the wolf could not free himself from it. But I did—using a sword that fights by itself, Unferth's gift, poison-twig mistletoe.

"The witch-hag, wilful woman, I conquered in her bleak bower. The troll-wench begged me, sword-wielding swain, to stay by her shameful side. I abandoned her, aching for more. Now she is a sad sprite, gone from our world, hale hall. The gladsome gleeman sings to us, she hears only the raucous raven's cry."

Wealhtheow was delighted to hear of the mere-wife's demise. Her sons' rival to the throne was dispatched as was the legal wife who could challenge her. Now she must plan for the future. Hrothgar was old and her sons not of age. "Beowulf," she pled, "do you vow to protect these boys, should they have need of your might?"

"Yes, lady," said Beowulf warmly, smiling deep into her

welcoming eyes. "I'll protect them should it ever be necessary." Then, in a voice no one could hear, "And you as well, I would shelter in my arms should you wish."

Wealhtheow did not break her gaze. She had more heir hope, kin care, than husband homage, consort covenant. So is it with women married to kings. She worried more for the future, than for the present age. She held out the cup, potion of promise.

That pledge would never be fulfilled.

Chapter 23

Re Member

In Heorot, the scop sang of the cannibal monster, the walker alone, seizing thirty thanes and drinking their boiling blood. Grendel would pay no wergild, rejecting compensation, dark demon of dim drear. Bold Beowulf conquered the kin of Cain, healing Heorot. Then the warlike wench, hateful whore, miserable monster mother, her terror less than her son's just as a woman is less strong than a man, avenged her ache on Æschere. Beowulf, brave in battle, mastered the mere and wasted her away in the waves. So sang the scop, metering Brimhild's life in mere words, aberrant alliteration, glib gleeman.

The Weder warriors celebrated several weeks. Wasted warriors vomited racy riddles.

A thirsty man may seek me out.
I can be sharp at first
and cold.
If you suck on me
I warm to your touch.
I start to melt, get wet with heat.

I pool from your touch
until consummation comes.

"I'm melting just hearing this riddle. Am I poking you, my dear," shouted one boorish brute, sitting a slave girl tight on his lap.

"I think the rhyme's riddle is your curly cunt!" cried another, grabbing her there.

The thanes joked with their thralls, pawing them publicly. That play was bitter to those women, coarse comrades' captives.

"The correct answer is," announced the puzzle poser, "an icicle."

"Bugger me if I don't have a filthy mind!" yelled a sailor with glee.

While Heorot rejoiced, Freawaru carried around mead, her cut arms wrapped in weavings, webs of woe. Never again would those white chains, now streaked with bloody scars, embrace the bold warrior. She was promised to Ingeld, son of Froda, slaughtered by the glory-Scyldings.

Later this marriage would weave peace, for a time. Freawaru's retainers came with her, to Ingeld's hall in the land of the Heathobards. Heathobard ring-treasures, presents from slaughtered warriors, hung on the Scylding belts. At ale-cups, one old fighter would ask Ingeld, "How can you let these Danish butchers get away with your father's killing? A good son avenges his father's death." Speeches like these would ring in Ingeld's ears nightly. Teasing can turn to strife, when too much mead is drunk. At last Freawaru's retainer would be hacked down in his sleep. Ingeld's love for his wife would transform into burning passion to destroy Heorot.

This had not yet happened when Freawaru walked in the gold hall. Gold-adorned and young, she thought only of her slaughtered pledge-partner.

Your darling body
mutilated, shamed, defiled.
It reemerges whole,
complete,
missing only your heart.
That I carry
in my breast;
mine nestles
within your ribcage.

At least I can still
re
member.

Brimhild carried her son, slaughtered by ruse, butchered by barbarians, to a promontory far from the fetid mere, swamp of stink. Here she placed him in an ancient barrow, scattered with bones. Though this was no love cave, that hero would not be lonely. Kissing his lips and bidding farewell, she laid him in a sleeping position. By his side she placed his work axe for cutting peat, along with a wooden copy of his sword she had fashioned from a branch. His true sword had been stolen by Beowulf. The grieving mother put a pot of food by his right hand, so he would not hunger in the afterworld. She tore off her necklace. The hammer ring and the amber bead scattered in the earth. Then she filled the entrance of the barrow with pieces of wood.

On top of the barrow she placed a cross and prayed. "Oh God, your truth these cagey killers are too blind to see. They love only violence and hide their foul deeds. My medicine, magical method, comes from the gods of the past. Odin, one-eyed wonder, is weakening, and the Christ is commencing to conquer. My home in the mere, morass of old ways, superstitious swamp, I vow to cleanse of heathen hate and endow with Mary's mirth. I bid you protect my slaughtered son, crucified Christ, butchered Baldr, sacred sacrifice, bitter to bear. Help me to praise you in my prayers, with my leech-lore."

Then she lit the wood aflame. The smoke rose to the sky.

The tears on her cheeks dried in the wind, cold and bone-gnawing. She stood up, aged in anger, ailing elder, wizened from woe.

Far off, a girl, frenzied Freawaru, saw that smoke. She spoke.

Your bone-house melts on flaming pyre.
Torn limb from limb, dissolved,

your body, which I caressed,
enters air, settles to ground.
If I throw myself upon that earth,
will you embrace me?
If I drink in deep draughts of breath,
will I inhale you?
Torn apart, will you
come together in me?
Disjointed, can I
re
member you?

Under the warming rays of the sun,
bony sea will melt.
Spring must come.

This once happened; so, too, this will pass.

IV. The Sea-Seer

This riddle, my personal experiencing, I put about my most melancholy self. I can tell what tribulations I have endured recently or of old since I grew up, and never more than now. I have suffered perpetually the misery of my exile's paths....When on account of my woeful plight I went wandering, a friendless exile.

The Wife's Lament

Husband, my husband, when will I glimpse your ring-carved prow over the horizon? You leave to fish the seas while I lure roots from the ground. We manage without you, beloved. But the boy needs you to teach him the honest ways of men, the girl needs you to admire and love. And I? Why, I need your warmth at night. My thighs grow cold, my belly's not blossoming. I wish for another child. You men who fish, out on the ocean, solitary sailor, far from home—what do you dream as you float along, seeking schools of prey, fleeing strange men in bigger boats with swords and axes? Do you think of us here with our little lives, clinging to the sand just where the sea-grass is rooted? We think of you staring at the grey tumbling waves. They splash in your face, freeze your beard, ache your hands which bleed when pulling ropes. You are my man—that is all that history will know.

Yet I have a past too. Once I was a child.

Chapter 24

The Charm of Life

Late 420's, Brimhild's cottage

A chill had settled on the mere. Icy rain splattered on the surface of the wintry well. Brimhild's earth-hut was warm. A peat fire burned on the hearth. Eel stew bubbled in the thick, blackened cauldron. Grease rose to the top, which Brimhild skimmed off and placed in a blue pot filled with hardened lard. One day it would prove useful for some sick soul.

A soft knock could be heard on the door. She no longer checked through the window. Beowulf had not reappeared. His boast that he had killed her had long been disbelieved. The time had passed since Hrothgar's people would come after her in vengeance. It was known she was still alive, eeking out her survival in this watery place. More than one hall dweller sought her out for medical help. She lay planks down on the bog so the sick could come to her home. Her magic—the way of women— was too powerful for her enemy's strong grip, his mighty muscles. Time had passed. Even the foul mere blossomed with the melting of winter ice. Yet today, spring pleasure lay months away.

Brimhild opened the door. A girl stood there, huddled in a thin woolen cloak, soaked from rain and tears. Brimhild could see she had come for a brew or potion. That was her place now, a lady-leech to the people of the Scyldings. Fisher folk and farmers, children and babes, women in birth bitterness, were brought to her for help. They made their way over the murderous mere to her healing hands. Some she helped, others no cure could save. She did what she could. They paid her with food, clothing, pots and pans, even manual labor. She never refused their presents, just as she never turned anyone away.

The girl, chilled to the bone, stumbled in. Brimhild poured out some soup in a cup. The girl drank it eagerly and seemed to warm up. Then she retched up the boiling beverage.

"I need your help," she whispered.

"Tell me, dear child," said Brimhild, wiping her brow with a cloth scented in herbs.

"I am with child. I must get rid of it." The young girl seemed desperate. Brimhild was not surprised. Many women came to her with just such a problem. Some she helped, others she sent away resigned to their plight. Lustful lovers who knew no control Brimhild counselled to keep the bairn as a love-pledge for the future. Women with too many children she gave concoctions to sever the male seed's service in future bed bliss. The humiliation of probing pirates, pitiful pawing, she resolved for many a sad-eyed maiden. The hour of shame should not have been. Scops tell of Princess Beadohild. She had no strength to strive against Weland, who made her big with child. The women Brimhild saw suffered their womb-woe, though no song sounds their sorrow.

"Tell me, my child. How old are you?"

"Fourteen winters, lady. I know you have helped some in the past."

"How far are you gone?"

"Eighty days."

"How came you to this state?"

"The Heathobards came. They raped my mother before me and took her away. After they humiliated me, I managed to escape. I've been too afraid to return home. I've lived in the reeds, eating fish raw and stealing what I could. I was lost for a time—then I remembered hearing of you. Help me, lady."

"Have you no family?"

"My father was taken in slavery. My younger brother as well. The whole village was burnt. Everyone was killed or enslaved."

"Did the king nothing?"

"I don't know. I don't care. What can he do now? It's too late for my loved ones. I'm alone, an exile, no one to care for me, no one for me to care for."

"You could keep the child."

"A child born of violence? I hate it. I want it dead."

"What is your name?"

"Edith, lady."

Brimhild considered for only a moment.

"Would you let me have your child, Edith?"

"What?"

"I could keep you here, feed you, and care for you. After the child is born, you may stay or go as you will."

"Why do you want this wretched thing?"

"I am lonely, my dear. My son died years ago. People visit me for help. No one stays for long. I have knowledge, useful wisdom. I can train your child, boy or girl, to learn the herbal way to help others. It would be a redemption of the hate hastened on you. You could help your people that way."

Edith thought for several moments.

"Don't decide yet, my dear. You are tired, sick, and hungry. Rest here a few days, eat what you can, and then decide what you should do."

Edith stayed several days. The days became weeks. Then she asked Brimhild, "May I be trained by you? I'm quick and I'm clean. I could be your helper, and the child could learn as well."

"I was hoping you would ask," Brimhild said smiling. "My work is for aiding the helpless and those in desperation. No matter how poor or how wealthy, illness and death comes to each one of us. While I can't prevent death, I sometimes make living less loathsome."

Edith observed and helped. She watched Brimhild as she dealt with the ill and injured. Brimhild taught her of the Disir, the female supernatural beings whose magic could help cure those in need. Edith learned of Gróa, wife of Aurvandil the

Brave, whose recitation over Thor cured his head. She heeded the seeress who told a wounded man to take a bull:

"Kill him on an elvish hill. Make that mound red with bull's blood. Feast with the elves on that fatty flesh. Soon will you be healed."

Sometimes they would leave the hut to attend to a patient too ailing to move. Edith watched babies being born. She hearkened how to cure women's weakness. To staunch women's blood, she would take comfrey or halswort, pounded into a dust, and have the woman drink it in wine. Or she would tell the suffering woman to take a comb with which she alone has combed, and which no other man has combed or ever shall comb. Under the morbeam tree, she should comb her hair, gathering that which is lost in the comb, and hang it on an upstanding twig. Then later, once the flux stops, she should gather the hairs from the tree and preserve them. These would be a leechdom for her.

If she continued to bleed too much, Edith would take fresh horse turds and lay them on hot coals. They had to smell strongly between the thighs, under her skirts, so that she would sweat much.

Edith performed the charm for women whose milk would not come in, threatening the life of the infant. Such a mother should pour the milk of a single-colored cow in her hand. That creamy concoction she should then drink up with her hand. Then the woman should go to running water, lively liquor, and spit that milk into the brook. Thereafter, ladling up with the same hand a mouthful of that water, she should swallow it. Finally, to cause the milk to stream forth from her breasts, she should say:

Wherever I walked, I went not alone.
The hero's son, mighty meat,
lay in my belly.
Now, I seek to claim myself and return home.

Once she has finished uttering these words, she should go to a house not her own and there taste meat. She should never look about as she carries out the charm. This way the charm will work and her milk will flow like the water in the flowing stream.

When her own lying-in came, Edith was prepared. A girl child was born. Edith named the babe after Brimhild's birthname, Sif.

That is my name.

Chapter 25

The Wyrd-Wife

I learned as a baby to avoid certain places by the mere and so, by the time I was six half-years in age, Brimhild and Edith let me wander about. The mere was no frightening fort for me, only a wonderland of strange plants and swimming serpents. I was a child of nature. All its aspects, foul and fearsome, awful and inspiring, were as one to me. I thrived in them all. Brimhild and Edith took me to the ocean to smell the clean salt air and touch the bracing ocean waves. I would spend long hours staring at the creamy waves, entranced by sea song. I drifted with the tide, spun spray stories.

The medical lore I mastered, just as I had walking and talking. I pretended to cook as all young children do. My dishes were poultices and salves. I even created creams and cures which Brimhild herself had not thought of. Spells I spoke like nursery stories, chanted curing rhymes. The pretty poppet was a neat nurse, diminutive doctor.

I called Brimhild "Grammy," just as Edith called her "Mother," for she had given her a second birth to life after the dismal death of despair. Brimhild told us stories from the past of woeful women.

"Hildeburh knew the paradox of loving—son and brother killed, both kin groups at war, battling bloodlines—peace poisoned and past. Sigrún wept when Helgi, fearless lover, killed her kinsman. Later she would curse her brother for murdering her marriage-mate. Hild's magic keeps dead warriors, fearless followers of her lover and those of her father, alive. That battle will continue until the Twilight of the Gods. One woman, beloved of Wulf, married to Eadwacer, was forced to endure anguished embrace, sorrowful separation, doleful difference. King

Antiochus, loving father, raped his daughter, polluted princess. He knew his own flesh and blood, kingly cannibal, royal ruffian. Helgi, dying, bid his heart-twin, Sváva, to marry his brother. She never would lie in the arms of that man of mettle, without fame. All of these women, sung of by scops, lurk in the lives of lauded lords. Scylding sirens sing of sorrow."

These tales, echoing from distant shores, whispered on the hut's hearth, in cottage's corners.

We three women lived on the edge of society, bunkered on borders. We were never alone for long. Wounds and illnesses cannot retreat forever.

One day, when I was twenty-four half-years, a knock could be heard. The hand which hammered knew no restraint. "Lady! Are you there?"

Brimhild opened up. She looked into the eyes of her father, her husband, her son.

It was Wealhtheow's offspring, a grown man of fifty half-years. "I am Hrothmund," he said.

"Welcome, sir. Seat yourself by the fire." My mother and I stood in the shadows, gazing at the stranger, bold in his boasting. "Sif, fetch a cup of broth for this gentleman. He has travelled a long journey."

"It is only a few hours away," he protested.

"It has taken you years to arrive." Brimhild looked at him calmly. "You know who I am?"

"Yes, lady. My father told me of his first concubine."

"I was his wife."

"Indeed. My mother is queen."

"I wish her a happier reign than mine."

"I come for your aid, lady. The queen is grievous sick."

"What ails her?"

"A pain in the heart. Though she cannot speak, she understands."

"That is true of most women at all times."

"You speak in riddles."

"Never mind, sir. I shall come. And my helpers as well. My daughter and granddaughter."

"Your daughter!" exclaimed Hrothmund in a shocked voice. "My father told me there had only been a son and he has been killed."

"Indeed. These are my adopted kin."

"Gather your medicines. I bid you not to tarry. My mother may not live much longer. I don't expect you to save her, only bring her ease. Perhaps she may speak again."

"Perhaps, sir."

We women gathered numerous dried herbals, pots filled with shimmering liquids, and salutary salves. We started off across the mere. "How did you find your way here?"

"When I was a boy, a hero stayed with us. Beowulf. He told of how the path to your hut could be conquered and how his best companion and my father's loyal retainer died in the murderous muck of the mere. He told, too, of your marvelous magic, how it overpowered his grasping grip, how the genius of giants guided your gestures. He said that you had died. I could not believe him. A brave man—brutish. A killer of cunning—not culture. Your son terrified our retainers. In me he aroused wonder. After all, he was my brother. Without a token of you, your arm, your head, your hair, a death is not proven. I resolved to return one day. "

"He was your half-brother."

"I did not want him dead."

"He is buried on the promontory over the beach. A cross marks his grim grave, purified by fire."

"So you are a Christian? Yet you practice magic."

"Medicine is not magic. God gave us nature to help us. If I try to honor God by utilizing his gifts, I'm a good Christian. It's true that some charms evoke Mother Earth and Odin. Their power still pervades these heathen climes. Are you a Christian?"

"No. Yet the pope's priests are as welcome as Odin's votresses.

Let us embrace both ways if they can be used."

Brimhild approved of her son's usurper. She sorrowed that they could not have been companions. Off we went to Heorot, her first trip there since she carried the head of Æschere in her grim grief at Grendel's going. Heorot looked battered, worn and dim. Tarnished and tattered, the once proud gold-hall was groaning and grave.

"Why is the happy hall so melancholy?" asked Brimhild. Edith and I huddled near her. Retainers looked up at us, stood in fear and anger.

"The queen's illness is just the latest of sorrows," said Hrothmund. "Beowulf promised to aid us as boys should we ever have need of his help. Hrothgar was betrayed by Hrothulf in this very hall several half-years ago. Hrothulf, my cousin, fatherless boy, was raised by Hrothgar—"

"And me."

"And you, lady, banished bewitcher, until you went. Then Wealhtheow was his foster-mother. He and Hrothgar held off Ingeld, faithless son-in-law. He broke the peace marriage with Freawaru and burned the hall. We repaired it without art and that oath breaker was killed. Hrothulf was a loyal foster-son.

"Yet Hrothulf harbored ambition. There was a time some seasons past, he spoke to my brother, Hrethric. Hrothulf spoke of Hrothgar's weeping at Beowulf's departure, called those tears Freya's gold. He said Hrothgar our father carried an unmanly affection for Beowulf in his heart. No man could ignore this taunt, insolent insult. Hrethric drew his glory-sword. Hrothulf's poison-twig was too potent for him. My brother lay dead. Hrothgar died an old man's grief.

"I came to Hrothulf, eager for glory. He welcomed my sword, said he loved death ever since his beloved Inga was killed. For her passing he hated Hrothgar, provoked revenge. I gave him what he wanted. His body then lay mute.

"Now the queen lies voiceless and still. Her presence could

hearten the weary-hearted heroes of Heorot one last time before the hall fires burn it utterly away. For now it awaits its final destruction from Heathobard hands."

"You know?" asked Brimhild.

"I have dreamed that a raging river swept into the hall, breaking its beams. A bear entered, destroying the gift-stool. He made us afraid. An eagle flew through, splashing us all with blood. These were my dreams."

"I, too," revealed Brimhild, "have seen the gold hall, melted and destroyed, by inner treason and alien encounter. Doughty degens will descend, burn the benches, engulf the gift-stool in flame. Your queen will speak once more, only to bid you and the life of hall-queen farewell. I know it all too well."

"Why do you help us, lady? I sense you would, yet why?"

"Your queen is innocent of my downfall, Hrothmund. It is her husband whose guilt needs be granted. His punishment comes in the end of his family, no heirs shall survive, the hall shall be twisted black beams and empty embers, decayed and deserted."

Hrothmund took Brimhild to the women's quarters. Wealhtheow lay on her pallet, pallid and pale, promising death. Her eyes saw Brimhild and acknowledged the agony committed on Grendel, soon to sever her own son.

Brimhild held out her hands and Edith and I swiftly pulled out medicinals. Brimhild chose several dried herbs and mixed them with a thick green substance. Then she brewed the concoction with water and fed it, hot, to the queen. "Now she must sleep," said Brimhild, ushering all out save herself.

"What if she kills the queen?" asked an aged retainer, whose memory of Brimhild's brilliance had not failed.

"She cannot," promised Hrothmund securely. "She knows what will happen and when. She cannot change it."

The night hours passed. At the first greying of light Wealhtheow opened her eyes. "Brimhild," she whispered, "Hrothgar never told me his secret with you, that he was your father. I had guessed in my heart. That knowledge kills me now."

"It has only killed my son. And my hope and love."

"You were hard done by."

"I made my choices how to live. Do not concern yourself with me. I have hung on by the edges and there I'll remain. You, in your glory, the center of Scyldings, the queen of a country, must face defeat and dread death in the once hope-filled hall."

Wealhtheow sang her last song.

Treachery abounds.
The sea boils
with ships and men
glad to betray,
eager for fame.

Only we women can
preserve the past
for future killers
and their pawns.
I pass around the cup,
laden with mead,
drink of the peace
promised by traitors,
poisoned by memory.

Her voice faded away as she swooned. Brimhild went to the door and summoned Hrothmund. "Now is the time to see your mother. Her time is near."

Hrothmund entered expectantly and Brimhild left them alone. Edith came to talk to her. "What will happen? I don't like it here. It seems so dismal and dank. I want to return to our hut, although it is small and rough. It has a warm fire."

"We will be home soon. This hall will be no more."

Before she returned to her hearth-hole, Brimhild spoke to

Hrothmund. "Your mother?"

"Dead. At peace. Unlike me."

"You must not forget, Hrothmund, though there is no hope. Your kingdom is doomed. It will pass away. The foreigner will come. You can heal your land. Perhaps not for now, but for the future. Tell this charm, the charm for unfruitful land. It may resurrect this ground in generations to come."

"You speak of magic lore, mere-woman. Yet I will say this, wyrd-wife." Later Hrothmund chanted and took up four turfs from the four quarters of the land. He took oil and honey and barm, and milk of each of the livestock which were on the land, and a piece of each species of tree which grew on the land and a portion of each plant of known name. He then put these in holy water which he dripped three times on the underside of the turfs. He said these words, "*Crescite*, grow, *et multiplicamini*, and multiply, *et replete*, and fill, *terre*, the earth. *In nomine patris et filii et spiritus sancti sit benedicti*." He said the Paternoster. Carrying the turfs to the church, he held them out. The priest sang four masses over them, the grass turned towards the altar. Later Hrothmund took a seed, setting it on the body of the plough and saying:

"Erce! Erce! Erce! Mother of earth! May the Ruler of all, the everlasting Lord, grant you fields sprouting and shooting, increasing and strengthening, tall stalks, shimmering crops and broad barley crops and glistening wheat crops and all the crops of the earth! May the everlasting Lord and his saints who are in the heavens grant him that his tilth be protected against any and every foe, and defended against each and every evil thing, from the witchcrafts sown across the land! Now I invoke the Ruler who shaped this world, that there be no woman so skilled in conjuration and no man so cunning that they may aver the words thus spoken."

Then he drove a plough forward and opened the first furrow and said, "Hale may you be, earth, mother of mortals! Grow pregnant in the embrace of God, filled with food for mortals' use." Then he said "*Crescite...in nomine patris...sit benedicti*" three times, and the Amen and the Paternoster three times.

Hrothmund did this. Hundreds of half-years later the magic would be good, after Hrothmund's bones had been picked clean by ravens.

Before Brimhild left, Hrothmund bid her farewell. "My mother told me your secret, lady, who your father was. It means our hall here is doomed. Wrongs don't go unavenged. Time makes sure of that."

Chapter 26

The Death Dirge

Brimhild lived many more half-years, sundry seasons. She continued to heal as she aged and withered. Edith and I mastered the art of herbal medicine through her guidance and training. Brimhild believed that the new ways should be kneaded into those of the old. She taught us the Nine Herbs Charm and how Odin learned the secrets of the magic runes while hanging, like Christ. So his legacy has helped man and woman against pain and disease. Brimhild warned me and Edith that some women put their daughters on roofs or in the oven to cure fevers. While this folk remedy might seem strange, she taught us to be sympathetic to the old ways. A child might be put on the roof to be cooled down. Or, as the oven cooled, so too would the child's fever. She cautioned us to be silent before the priests who started to enter the land. They punished women who tasted their husbands' blood as a remedy, when sometimes that was the only cure.

Edith and I learned many recipes to help peasants, farmers, and sailors. Some were for bothersome problems. For the man whose wife chatters too much, we were told he should taste at night, while fasting, a radish root. That day the chatter cannot harm him. There were charms for life-threatening disease. Brimhild's daughter and I, her granddaughter, her adopted flesh, learned aid runes, which grant help bringing the child from the mother. The runes we cut in our hands, then held the hand of the laboring mother, bidding the guardian spirits not to fail. We learned the branch runes, to heal and understand wounds. These runes we cut on trees with east-leaning branches. The day came when our training was vital.

Season after season slipped away.

Over the moor came mutilated men, savaged by swords, bloodied with blades. They were carried by comrades, fearless fellows, to the healing hut. Brimhild came out of retirement, so labored were her daughters. For head wounds, we took betony, rubbing it into dust. The ailing swallowed it in hot beer, healing the broken crown. Oft times we took waybread or plantain seed, sowing it into the wound, making the body whole. For bruises, Brimhild recommended hart clover, pounded in a wooden vessel, and drunk in wine. Or else we would pound rosemary with lard and lay it on the wound.

Some soldiers had been burned, harmed by Heathobards. Fiveleaf the herb cured them. "To make a different salve," instructed Brimhild, "burn goat's turd and straw to dust, then mix it with butter and boil well. Strain that soup through a cloth and smear on the charred flesh."

Despite those cured with leechdoms, there was no end of failed physic. Putrid gangrene consumed one living corpse, quick carrion. The enemy contaminated the water, delivering a mortal mead to the Scyldings. Then old and young crossed the murky mere. "Do not drink that fatal fluid, lethal liquid," warned Edith to the common folk. "For diarrhea, pound cinqfoil, brooklime, churmel, and lupin. Then boil them in milk. You must drink it in the morning and at night." The feverish drank betony.

Some of the sick survived, those whom fate had ordained long lives. Others had no promise of pleasure, only the anguish of ache. They relished release. Brimhild even practiced trepanning, cut into hard skull with a sharp flint knife. Sometimes that warrior's head would heal, though ofttimes that brain was bruised.

One warrior was led to their nursing nest. He had swollen eyes, injured in battle. Brimhild held a live crab, took its eyes out, and put it alive again in the water. Then she put the eyes on the neck of the man. "You will soon be well," she promised the thane.

One girl not yet grown, yet no longer a child, arrived, maddened with misery. Blood dripped down her legs. So she would not bear fruit against her will, Edith boiled brooklime in ale. The girl drank the potion while bathing in a hot bath. Then Edith made a poultice of beer dregs, green mugwort, marche, and barley meal. These she mixed together. She shook them up in a pan and applied to the girl's vulva after her bath. The girl drank the warm brew again and was wrapped up well, poulticed for a long time of the day. She was no longer able to speak, struck dumb by her encounter. Edith took pennyroyal dust and wound it up in wool. The girl slept on it, and woke up cured. She bore no offspring from her encounter, save those in her dreams and tortured thoughts.

A hairy brute approached, laced with blood. I examined him.

"You're a beautiful girl," this man remarked.

"Your eyes are clouded with blood."

"My vision is perfectly fine."

I raised my eyebrows and swiftly glanced at him. "Your timing isn't."

He laughed, then caught himself short with a gasp of pain.

"Where does it hurt?" I asked.

He motioned to his left side.

I thought it prudent that I not heal this impudent fellow. "Mother! This man needs you."

"No, lady, I need you." He smiled through the pain. I had to admire his boldness.

"My mother will heal you."

"Only you can heal the wound you've inflicted."

This time I laughed. "You men kill, get covered in red hot gore, and yet can flirt with your healers?"

My mother poked him in the ribs—to see if they were only bruised or broken and to remind him of her presence. He swore.

"Look, you," said Edith, "we women patch you savages together to go back and wreak more havoc. Then you return with more wounds and go back to kill some more. One day, none of you will return for healing."

"The day that happens is our day of victory," he smiled.

"The day that happens is the day of this nation's doom," replied Edith.

He seemed to reflect on this as Edith wound a bandage tightly around his middle.

"You've only bruised those bones. There now," said Edith, tying off the cloth, "go kill some more live ones."

"Here, now, mother," he began respectfully, "what else is a man to do? Let these aliens come and take over, sell you and your daughter to the highest bidder? Surely you wish us success."

"I wish for peace."

"It comes only when my blade is faster and cuts more deeply than the other fellow's. I fight for you."

"You fight for the pleasure of killing."

"Mother!" I interrupted. "He is right. If Heorot falls, so do we."

"Then off with you," said Edith bitterly. "Be a brave man and impress my foolish daughter."

He took another look at me. It was so penetrating, my breath stopped for an instant. He left the tent and I exhaled once again. I turned to my mother. "How could you goad him? He's right, much as we hate it. Only if he kills well can we survive."

"Those ribs hurt wickedly. They'll slow him down." Edith smiled. "I know men. I've angered him. He'll fight all the harder to prove himself to me. After all, I'm the mother of the girl he fancies, for today."

The hard work of healing weakened my grandmother. Yet Brimhild clung on that season, lady leech by the lake. Aged and ailing, she suffered aches in her joints. She bid Edith invoke the Valkyries, warrior women, to ease the stitch in her bones. Her daughter spoke, chanted the magic incantation, marvel maxim:

Loud were they, lo! loud
when over the hill they rode:
shield thee now that you may survive their ill-will.
Out little spear, if you are in here!
I stood under the linden wood,
under a light shield,
where the mighty women
their main strength proved.
And screaming they sent forth their spears.
Out spear; not in, spear!
If herein there be, of iron a bit,
the work of hags,
it shall melt.
Whether you have been shot in the skin,
or shot in the flesh,
or shot in the bone,
or shot in the limb,
may your life never be endangered.
This as your remedy for the shot of Æsir,
this for the shot of elves,
this for the shot of witches,
I will help thee.
Fly to the mountain head.
Be whole.
May the Lord help thee!

Then Edith took the knife she had pointed with and put it into liquid.

After the charm was uttered, Brimhild spoke wryly, "The Valkyries take the dead warriors to Valhalla. Worthy women, wonder-wives, they can shoot pain here on earth."

That last night, the eve of the final battle, Brimhild lay fast by the fire. In its glowing light, she saw the past and future, the doom of Danes. The fates she fathomed, whelming wyrd. She chanted her death dirge, singing sorrow.

"Once on the wintry tide, I floated ashore, a babe baptized by salt water, abandoned, then found. Alien anger anchored me in my anguish. I am the repository of woman's plight, the fortune of female, the wit of the womb. My mother humiliated, the lowest of lusts lay in her loins. A king who conquers cunts, vanquishes vulvas, will be avenged by the womb's warrior.

"The bard tells us that in ancient days, a king named Priam had fifty sons and fifty daughters. His grandson, Odin, settled the northlands where we abide. Priam's daughter, Cassandra, bore a daughter who fled north. Her name was Erda. She could see all and know all. Unlike her mother, her words were received as wisdom and prophetic truth. Her daughters' daughters' daughters still utter mystic murmurings. The foremother's curse has been revived. She is heard no more. Dismissed as foolish or mad, the wavy-haired woman sings her lament, of slavery, humiliation, and death. Her words waft heavenwards, drifting like smoke, impotent and invisible in the sky.

"The scop's song still is sung. He sings of the hero's exploits, the warrior's wandering, the attacker's act. The killer is sung as an avenger, the pirate's a tribute-seeker, the rapist a good king. Only the peaceweaver is sung of with praise, her cup a tapestry doomed to unravel, her words of welcome weak. The seer's song is unrecorded, shunned by the meadhall, sacred only to shore and mere, heard by the curlew, wafting to whale, sunk into the sea. The hero's triumph overshadows the woman's truth. She records history, witnesses world woe. That lady lulls in a lullaby lowly, whispering the ways of woman, the seeress's sorrow, prophetic past. Children alone, innocent babes, know her story, lapping their minds like light from ceremony lamps. Then ritual erases the knowledge of nannies, memory of mother.

"What do women know? The heat of hearth, the mirth of the meadhall, the secrets of the sea, the worries of water, the scent of seaweed, the moo of milkcow, the mire of muck, the pain of periods, the boldness of blood, the lust of lovers, the lamentation of loss, the sorrow of sickness, the health in herbals, the hatred of heroes, the wrong of rape, the babbling of babes, the cheer of children, the echo of ecstasy, the anguish of avenging, the righteousness of revenge, the despair of disbelief, the hope of healing, the delight of daughters, the smile of sons, the dirge of daughters, the sadness of sons, the heartiness of husbands, the longing for lovers, the poignancy of peaceweaving, the lurching of loyalties, the desire for death—all this women know, and more."

Brimhild then sang her own life song, the story of her sadness. From birth to this moment, she shared her past. Brimhild paused, told of her enemy's fate.

"The loss of Beowulf's close comrade, drowned in the dreck of the murderous mere, killed in the marauder any love or affection. No wife for this woman-hater, no heir for the hero of hate. He returned to his lord's hall. After Beowulf returned home, Hygd, his king's wife, would sing of violated vows.

Before his lord, my husband,
he murmured
tender nonsense,
senseless mutterings
in my ear,
warm with his breath.

I hate that youth
for his youth
for his bold ways
for his foolishness.

He gave me that shining torque.
His hands laid it against my skin.
They lingered on my white flesh.

My bosom is warm.

"That lady did not feel the hero's heat again. Beowulf was determined to scorn the swollen-bellied bride. So he fates his folk to alien acquisition after his agony. Across the sea Beowulf now battles, abandoned by all save Wiglaf, eager for fame. Beowulf sings his own sorrow, the Geats yielding to Swedish sailors.

O listen, you gods,
I'm angry with you,
my wretched end is nigh.
Now enemies come,
pull boats on shingle.
The dune is breached.
My only posterity
is my name.
O how my people will suffer!

I die without
heir or son.
My people fear the worst.
No child have I
to carry my honor
after bone-rings burst.
My only posterity
is my name.
O how my people will suffer!

Now they're here,
hold me tight
in white-hot clasp.
My people lament,
removed to remote realm.
Disaster does not delay.

My only posterity
is my name.
O how my people will suffer!

That enemy's violence cannot save his nation. He must sing a mournful elegy."

Brimhild chanted her last lament.

"The tune of our land is also plaintive and grave. Even so, Froði's peace was destroyed. The seer sings of sorrows, heard only by nature, a whisper in the reeds, ignored by man. The warrior wields his weapon, the phallus of fear or the blade, bloody and blunt. The peace-weaver praises while passing the cup, drinking bitter brew and melancholy mead.

"Alien enemies will wash ashore, there is no end. Pillaging and plundering, humiliating and humbling, willful warriors will invade our peoples, my adopted land. My mother's kin, the jealous Jutes, will likewise be brought low by the pirates from abroad, northern navigators. Here the Heathobards come. Then new tribes will conquer the enemies of the Scyldings. Hale heath heroes will harass halls, gone will be golden gables, bone-rings will burst in the blaze. Many hundred half-years will pass until one king will conquer. No good king, yet a tenacious tyrant will hold sway over many peoples. Doughty degens, keen killers, will continue to storm the beaches, wading the whale's path, to claim kins' country. The cries of children and the tears of women will be the legacy of wanton warriors.

"Brother kills brother. Sisters' sons slaughter spindle and spear kin. Incest bears rotten fruit. Ragnarök beckons, ravenous wolves devour the sun. Ice melts. Fire destroys. Venom drips on Loki. His wife catches it in a basin. When the basin fills, she empties it. While she is gone, the poison falls. Loki trembles. Quakes shudder the land. Earth shall be torn asunder, and high heaven.

"Eve, innocent icon, duped by the demon, feasting on fruit,

defying her Deity, gleaming with gold. Judith—joyous Jew—killing Holofernes, foul fiend and Hebrew hater. Salome, lustful lady, beheading gentle John. Only Christian consorts can save us now. Juliana, murdered martyr, savaging Satan and demolishing demons, converting her cousins to Christ. Elene, Constantine's mother, uncovering Christ's cross, jabbing at Judas, noticing nails, weeping with wonder, fainting for faith. Only in mirthful Mary, loving her son, leech of love, can our way find hope in this hallowed hall called earth, teeming with tyrants, robbers of ruth, groaning without grace.

"The best way is both ways, the strength of the past embracing the mercy of the future. Few will see the sense of that. They erase their mothers' wisdom, stomp out the seeress's sighs, close off the clever covenant. The daughters of Cassandra will melt away, returning as the maidens of Mary. A few will trace runic ruins, make manifest their manifold knowledge, for the help of humankind.

"Baldr and Jesus, blissful brothers, they will come to rescue us after the deluge, the conflagration. There we all will live, save those the Midgard Serpent, corpse-devourer, wings to his nest, loathsome lair. The land will be fruitful again, happy harvest, gleaming grain, lush land. Children will be born. They will not enter slavery. The sick will be salved, the sad soothed, the low lauded. A hall will be built, beauteous building, glorious gold, heavenly hall, joyful joinings. That is a good home!"

Brimhild closed her lips, never to open them again. With her last strength, she stood to overlook the mere. A pregnant red moon, streaked with grey, hovered heavily over the horizon, sucking in to itself the still night. The mere reflected a bloody blaze, rippling and ruffled by the breeze. To the beach she weakly walked, abandoning the noxious and noisome morass for the clean tang of the sea. Edith and I followed, guiding her faltering footsteps. Brimhild watched the moon, wounded and wandering, sink into the seals' home. Sighing her last song, she swooned into her death, fainting with fatigue, opening into oblivion.

We wove a boat coffin from the reeds, tightly wound tough fibers to fashion a floating nest. We wrapped Brimhild in a ghostly gauze. To her lips we held a fragrant flower, to make her entry into Valhalla favorable. Incense we daubed to ease her way to heaven, kindled her corpse. Glowing embers consumed her ancient bones. Laments we sang for mother, granddame, healer, seer, repository of the old way and the new, woman of Odin, guide to God, follower of Freya, maid of Mary.

The tide carried her, last of the old, the first of the new, flood's follower, ebb's martyr. Bone-rings burst in the blaze. Aching anguish abandoned, Brimhild's ashes mingle with the heavy seawater, sink to the sands, dissolve into dust, wash up on alien shore. There, an artisan, the last of the Roman-trained masters, gathers those grains to heat into a glimmering glow, glazing a glass. Glittering gold encircle the drinking horn of dark blue glass, beautiful beaker. Engraved with runestaves, ornamented with snakes, the costly cup tells of the World Ash, suffering tree. It holds the hanging Odin, eager to win rune lore; it embraces Christ when all creation weeps.

This glory goblet a peacebride passes, weaving a tapestry of calm, the healing of hope. Placing their lips to the cup, warriors utter their vows of peace. Then one, having drunk too much from the cup, provokes his neighbor, tenuous tether, breaking the brotherhood. He vanquishes the vessel, shattered and crushed in the humbled hall by the hero's heel. The men are noisy, deafening death, as if Baldr were returning to the hall, the dead kings feasting in Valhalla. Ale mixes with blood, gold with red, metal of strife with dew of wounds.

This once happened; so, too, this will pass.

V. The Undiscovered Country

A. D. 449. In this year John the Baptist showed his head to two monks who came from the east to worship in Jerusalem, at a place which once was Herod's residence. At that same time Marcian and Valentinian reigned; and at that time came the Angles to this land of Britain, invited by king Vortigern, to help him overcome his enemies. They came to Britain with three warships, and their leaders were Hengest and Horsa. First of all they slew the enemies of the king and drove them away, and afterwards they turned against the king and against the Britons and destroyed them by fire and by the edge of the sword....Their leaders were two brothers, Hengest and Horsa; they were sons of Wihtgils. Wihtgils was the son of Witta, the son of Wecta, the son of Woden; from this Woden sprang all our royal family.

The Anglo-Saxon Chronicle

My husband is a killer. Or was. Now he is a fisherman. Once he held sway in a hall, wielding weapons. Each woman hopes her man is a good killer. The whole nation depends upon men whose sword-blades drip with blood before other men redden their own.

Chapter 27

This Once Happened

440's, collapsed Scylding empire

The air was acrid. Along the hazy horizon unfurled smoke standards, pitch pennants. Golden gables gleamed in the licking light.

Heorot burned.

I have heard how Hrothmund fought against enemies. Valiantly he struck out with savage sword. Fate never saves the wyrd-wasted man though his courage may be good. That young warrior leaned on his final follower, single servitor. All others had deserted him, abandoned the Danish king for the enemy, faithless foe. He was hot with typhus fever. I made him a salve. I took bishopwort, lupin, viper's bugloss, strawberry plant, the cloved wenwort, earth rime, blackberry, pennyroyal, and wormwood. I pounded all the worts, boiled them in good butter, wrung through a cloth. After this I set them under the altar and bade the priest sing nine masses over them. I then smeared Hrothmund with the salve on the temples, and above the eyes, and above the head, and the breast, and the sides under the arms. This salve is also good for every temptation of the fiend, and for a man full of elfin tricks. Despite these efforts, Hrothgar's only living heir suffered an obscure end, debased death, abject agony.

Those fierce foreigners overwhelmed the remaining retainers. The hall crumbled, the kings of Scylding folk died off. Pirates oppressed the people and Heathobards came to conquer, vicious vanquishers.

The waning of the battle spelled our doom. We saw the fingers of smoke uncurl into the sky and mingle with the black fume from Brimhild's funeral boat. Death was everywhere.

It was time for us to flee. I grabbed our precious goods, gold and jewelry. Edith gathered some herbs and food. Just as we went to cross the threshold for one final time, a heavy step could be heard outside. We looked at one another and dove under the bed. Then a voice.

"Lady? Mother? Are you there?"

I crawled out and opened the door. That wounded soldier who had flirted with me was back.

"Lady! You are hale! You and your mother must leave at once. All is lost. The Scyldings are defeated. That kingdom is no more."

Edith stood behind me. "We know not where to flee."

"I have a ship. A group of us will make for the open water and then decide our fate."

We had no choice. We gambled that this warrior would not dishonor us. At least he was a killer from our side, not theirs. We made our way over the mere, and through the rushes. Then we raced along to the beach as quickly as we could go.

The longship was pulled up onto the shingle. Six men were waiting. Once they caught sight of us, they began to push the vessel into the water. Our fighter lifted us in the ship. And none too soon. For once we had left the shore, a mass of angry warriors appeared. They were not dressed as Scyldings are. The Scylding men rowed fiercely and we disappeared into the mist.

We sailed for several days. The men had brought water. Edith's food was divided up none too fairly, though it was true the men did all the rowing. They felt they were doing us a favor, so we did not to feel sensitive about how they treated us. Luckily our killer was their leader. He did not let them harm us.

They sailed around the mainland peninsula. Our man knew of a place, he said, peaceful and isolated. We landed. No one appeared to confront us, ask us our business. It was an empty landscape. We waded in from the shallows, our skirts heavy with sea water. In from the beach we made our way. A village was in a shambles, houses burned.

I knew then how our leader had chosen this spot. It was the scene of a recent Scylding triumph, the defeat of enemies, wanton destruction of families and fisherfolk. So nations are won and lost.

It proved to be a safe haven for us. He and his brother ordered the men. They all worked for days to build a shelter out of the remnants of a cottage tight by the sea. Edith and I scavenged for food. Though most of it was rotten, we found some root vegetables still edible. We fished as well.

Luckily it was spring. The warm weather meant our lack of clothes was not so dire. There was time to barter for goods before cruel winter set in.

Once a party of men came nosing around. Our leader greeted them. It seemed the grandfather of our killer-carer had eliminated an enemy of the father of one of their party, so all was well. They were Angles.

Edith and I cooked and kept house. We fished and tried to make the land fruitful. The men visited the lord's hall in twos and threes, never leaving us without a guard.

"Aren't you bored?" I taunted our leader one day. "Wouldn't you rather be killing?"

He was fishing as I wove a basket from reeds.

"No!" he laughed, "I like fishing perfectly well. It is more pleasant to fish for sea creatures than men who may puncture my bonehouse."

"Don't you miss the destruction?" I teased.

He looked serious. "Lady, do not make light of death. I have killed many men. Do you think I forget them? Everyday I reflect on them, faces float before my eyes. I see them gaze back at me. I had to slaughter. I feel no remorse. Yet they are part of me. Their blood mingles with mine own. They are my blood brothers."

A fish leapt onto his line. "You're a healer, you've seen death. I'm sure not all your patients lived. Don't you recall those who shuddered their last gasp, begging for help from the pain?" I shut my eyes, sickened by such memories. "I am no heartless attacker, Sif. I have feelings and dreams. One is to win you. You scorn me for my deeds. To my lord, I was a loyal hero. To you, I am an abomination, an awful atrocity."

I did not speak for several moments. "Can you change?" I asked.

"Change?"

"Give up killing?"

"I have not killed a man for four months!" he bragged and laughed at his mock boast. Then he was serious again. "Do you wish me to become other than what I am?"

"You like fishing, you say."

"Yes, I like fishing. Only it disturbs me to remember those deaths. The quietness of fishing makes me dwell on the past."

"Do you want to join this lord in his hall, fight for him?"

"No, lady. I want to join you in this hall," he pointed to the hovel, "play with you." The last was said in a low tone that made my skin redden with warmth.

"I will think on it," I promised.

"Sif," he said getting up, "I want a normal life. What is that to me? A wife and children. A normal life for many men is drunken boredom in the hall, and killing to protect that satiating pleasure. It was normal for me to rampage and slaughter. For you, healing is normal. Such is life. I do not agree with those who claim our lives are preordained by fate. Once I did. I thought my time was allotted me. If I were doomed to die, no amount of restraint would save me. If wyrd decreed I live, no amount of foolhardy behavior could harm me. So I fought foolishly, magnificently. I was a success."

"When did you stop believing in fate?"

"I believe in fate. Don't misunderstand me. I trust in the fate I fashion for myself."

"How do you create it yourself? Your lord gives you a fate.

You are given a place at court or the job of cowherd. It is difficult to change that."

"Though not impossible! I can become a fisherman if I choose."

I wondered about that. Could a man leave a life of destruction for one of placid water harvest?

I told him over the next few weeks of Christ. "Christ chose his fate, wove his destiny."

"No, he didn't," he cried. "He foolishly adhered to his Father's ways. If this man were a god, he surely should have seen that a future lay in defeating death, not agreeing to it."

"He did defeat death," I protested, "by dying."

He laughed. "Your riddles cannot sway me. That path does not lead to freedom. I've been forced to be another man all my life. Now I want to be my own."

"And how will you do that?" I asked coolly, upset he rejected the religion which appealed most to me.

"By starting out as a fisherman, husband, father. We'll see what happens from there." He held open his arms.

I capitulated, a victim of his virility, a captive to his words.

Now we have two children, a third on the way. My mother lives with us, caring for the cottage and the garden. His brother and the other soldiers have gone to court. Some have married. We still argue about freedom.

"You are free as a fisherman. No one tells you what to do," I argued.

"You do," he said as I laughed. "And your mother."

I ignored his joke. "Our lord has not summoned you. We give him some of your catch. Is that so bad?"

"It's not so bad," he agreed. "It proves we aren't free. The lowest of the low and the highest of the high are trapped."

"By what? How can a lord or king be trapped?"

"By the past, tradition, expectation, hope, and rivalry. He's worse off than a slave!"

"And we, what are we trapped by?"

"Each other, delicious love."

"There are ways to be free. I feel free when I gaze at the sea for minutes on end. Also when I pray to God."

"The only way to break free is to try a new land."

"A new land? Why can't you just be free where you are? You're always yearning, restless."

"I want to start fresh. Go abroad."

"We are abroad," I say bitterly. "Besides, men conquer and go abroad all the time."

"They don't change. I mean conquer, assimilate, and change. For the better."

"Men will never be better. Only women."

"Women? Oh, yes!" He laughed. "Women are fated. You have breasts and wombs. That is what is significant about you."

"Thank you," I said hotly.

"Mead maiden, I love you for your womanliness. And more."

"As a Christian soul I choose my own fate."

"Ha! Can you show me your soul? Christianity is an elvish story for slaves and women who have no hope in their lives. I don't blame you. I welcome you to it. I say freedom lies in a new land, to the west."

"The west? And then, in one hundred half years, your son's son will be sick of the nation you build. Where will he go?"

"He'll follow the sun. All men do."

"And how will you get this land? By conquering and killing?" I ask. We'd had this argument dozens of time. This is the first time he had brought up moving westward.

"Not killing. Living with. Seeing more of life than this blasted beach which has never changed and never will."

"Its colors are never once the same," I pointed out. "They flicker and alter constantly."

"My love for you never does." He embraced me tightly.

I felt a chill. "What are you planning?"

"You know our lord asked me last winter to become a mercenary. I turned it down. I want what's best for us, for our children." He looked out at the horizon. "We will go west in the spring, to a new land. It is fertile, I have heard, and the people cowardly. We need not kill them. We could live amongst them. There we can build a nation where each man—and woman, if you will—can make his own way, not trapped by tradition and gods. They darken the present. Why should I care what Odin did or what Thor wrought? They are nothing to me."

"They are the foundation upon which all that is glorious and traditional in our world is built, the myths and stories."

"They are the foundation of everything in our culture which is bloody awful."

"What nation can you build? One without gods?"

"I don't know. If I knew, I wouldn't want it. I like surprises. Life should be full of them, not grim chatterings of fate. Come, build it with me."

After a pause, I took my husband's hand and looked out over the calm grey sea to the west.

"I'll come, Hengest," I replied. The waves churned, white-capped with the rising wind. It was a choppy sea.

I have sung this lay, wrought this riddle, to preserve the past, understand the present, change the future. Now we've left our old fate, an empty husk, on the crumbling shores of what was. The sandy beach of this fair island is where we will forge our new fate. Will those who follow also fashion their own freedom?

This once happened; so, too, this will pass.

Note to the Reader

This book is based on *Beowulf*, a work that exists in a sole manuscript called Cotton Vitellius A XV, housed at the British Library. It dates from around 1000 and was partially destroyed by fire in 1731. That we have it at all attests to the tenaciousness of both the manuscript itself and scholars interested in preserving it. There continues to be much debate about the dating of the original version of *Beowulf*, since it is generally assumed by scholars that the one text we have is a late version of a poem originally orally composed.

It is often said that *Beowulf* represents the first, great epic in the (Old) English language, yet none of the action is set in England. It is set on the continent, mainly in Denmark and Sweden, during the migration to England by the Angles, Saxons, Jutes, and Frisians. Fred Robinson (Godden and Lapidge, 143) has suggested that Beowulf would have been born near the end of the fifth century and died late in the sixth century. This means that the poet(s) would have been looking back on the action in the poem from a distance of hundreds of years.

The action of the poem is well-known. It has three major sections: Beowulf's encounter with Grendel, Beowulf's encounter with Grendel's mother, and Beowulf's encounter with the dragon, bringing about the hero's death. The first two encounters take place when Beowulf is a young man and in the land of the Scyldings, ruled by Hrothgar. The fatal encounter takes place after Beowulf has ruled the Geats for fifty years.

Grendel's Mother is not the first creative response to Beowulf. There have been other such works, most famously John Gardner's *Grendel*. It, too, uses *Beowulf* as its source text. *Grendel* "talks" to Beowulf, but does not rely on the reader's knowledge of that work for readers to enjoy or understand the modern work. For those who know *Beowulf* well, many allusions in my book will be familiar to them. For those who have not yet read the Old English work, in the original or translation, my book is self-standing. My hope is that more people will read and love *Beowulf* and other works written in Old English. I have included a bibliography for readers to find handy translations of these wonderful poems, as well as those sources I have consulted.

As is evident from the title, my book reads the *Beowulf* story from the point of view of Grendel's mother. What do we know of her? In *Beowulf*, we first encounter her after Grendel's death, which she avenges by entering Heorot and killing Æschere. Then Hrothgar tells Beowulf about her. In Kevin Crossley-Holland's translation, the passage reads as follows: "The wandering, murderous monster slew him/ in Heorot; and I do not know where that ghoul,/ drooling at her feast of flesh and blood,/ made off afterwards. She has avenged her son....now another mighty/ evil ravager has come to avenge her kinsman....I have heard my people say,/ men of this country, counsellors in the hall,/ that they have seen two such beings,/ equally monstrous,/ rangers of the fell-country,/ rulers of the moors; and these men assert/ that so far as they can see one bears/ a likeness to a woman....These two live/ in a little-known country, wolf-slopes, windswept headlands,/ perilous paths across the boggy moors, where a mountain stream/ plunges under mist-covered cliffs,/ rushes through a fissure" (84-85). Beowulf swims all day to get to her home underneath a snake-infested lake. They fight, his sword powerless against her. His corselet protects him when she is about to stab him. Then he sees a sword made by giants; this enables him to behead her. He beheads the already dead Grendel with that sword, whose blade melts after encountering the monster's blood. Beowulf returns with Grendel's head and everyone celebrates.

I clearly used some of this material in my story. However, in my version, Grendel's mother does not die. Her death is just one of the many false tales told about her. I tried to include different aspects of Anglo-Saxon womanhood for her: child, wife, mother, hall-queen, avenger of kin, medical provider, seeress. I have adapted medical material and charms from Bald's Leechbook, as well as Bradley, Davidson, Singer, Swanton, and Weston. Do not try these recipes at home! Some of them I amended; they are not for personal use. The material about the Angel of Death is from Cohat.

I echo the Old English alliterative use of words present in Anglo-Saxon poetry. This consists of variation, that is, a noun or verbal phrase echoing or complimenting a noun or verb already stated, often representing an additional aspect of that concept. *Beowulf* is paratactic in style, which means there are very few coordinating conjunctions, unlike modern English which is hypotactic. My work is a mix of the two. It is difficult to write a work in modern English and be utterly paratactic. This work is not an Old English poem; it is a modern novel presenting the Anglo-Saxon material from a character's point of view. I have used aspects of Old English poetic verse craft, but have not been enslaved by them. Also, as Lee Hollander has discussed, it is virtually impossible to render a work in an entirely Germanic vocabulary for such frequently used words as battle, glory, revenge, etc. (Hollander, xxviii). Therefore, I have not purposely avoided Latin or French based words, though I have tried to include Germanic ones wherever possible.

Another aspect to *Beowulf* concerns the so-called "digressions;" that is, allusions in the midst of the main "plot" to events which happened elsewhere and previously, and even, as in the case of Beowulf's ruminations on Freawaru's marriage, in the future. These moments refer to heroes and figures from the Germanic and Nordic world, such as Sigemund or the bad king Heremod. This is part of the *Beowulf* poet's creative fashioning. The connection between a brief allusion and the main action must be teased out by the reader. I have incorporated numerous such moments from Germanic and Norse myth and history, trying to give enough context to allow the reader to make connections between main action and allusion. I have included a list of proper names, with source works, for those readers interested in finding out more about the figures alluded to. Much of that material comes from *The Prose Edda* by Snorri Sturluson (translated by Jean I. Young), *The Saga of the Volsungs* (translated by Jesse L. Byock), *The Poetic Edda* (translated by Lee M. Hollander), and *Gods and Myths of Northern Europe* (H. R. Ellis Davidson). I used both Nordic and Germanic allusions since the cultures were, at the time of *Beowulf*'s action (fifth-sixth centuries), so porous and interactive that I imagine the stories and gods would have been mutually known. I have set the story about one century earlier than the usual dating of the action for dramatic purposes.

This book was first inspired in the late 1990s by those enthusiastic hearth companions in my class "Anglo-Saxon Language, Literature, and Culture." I am grateful to all the students over the years whose wise and witty remarks have engendered a creative atmosphere motivating me to undertake a quest on Grendel's mother's behalf. I would also like to thank those who supported my creative work: Jane Chance, Haruko Momma, Candace Robb, Geoffrey Russom Robert T. Tally, Jr., Jane Toswell, and Bonnie Wheeler. Loving thanks as always to my husband, Jim Kilfoyle, children Sarah and John, and my parents, Robert and Joan Morrison.

Please visit the website of this book at grendelsmotherthenovel.com. There you may contact the author, follow her blog, and find information, including how to integrate this text into the classroom.

Sources for Quotes

1. *Cuckoo* (adapted from Boswell, 215).
2. *Apollonius of Tyre* (Swanton, 236). The Priest's speech to Mother Nature is adapted from Singer, xxxi; the sparrow story comes from Bede (Sherley-Price, 129-130); how Jerome cleanses the pagan temples comes from Pope Gregory's message to Augustine, missionary to the Anglo-Saxons, in 601 (Sherley-Price, 92).
3. Riddle 69 (Bradley, 404).
4. *The Wife's Lament* (Bradley, 384-5). Medical material comes from Cockayne [*Bald's Leechbook*], as well as Bradley, Davidson, Singer, Swanton, and Weston.
5. *Anglo-Saxon Chronicle* (Garmondsway, 12-13).

Bibliography

Bede the Venerable. *Ecclesiastical History of the English People.* Leo Sherley-Price, Trans. Harmondsworth: Penguin, 1955.

Boswell, John. *The Kindness of Strangers.* New York: Vintage Books, 1988.

Bradley, S.A.J., ed. *Anglo-Saxon Poetry.* London: J. M. Dent & Sons Ltd, 1982.

Byock, Jesse L., trans. *The Saga of the Volsungs: The Norse Epic of Sigurd the Dragon Slayer.* Berkeley: University of California Press, 1990.

Cockayne, Thomas Oswald, ed. and trans. *Leechdoms, wortcunning, and starcraft of Early England.* London: Holland Press, 1961. Volumes 1-3. [*Bald's Leechbook*]

Chickering, Howell D., Jr. *Beowulf: A Dual-Language Edition.* New York: Anchorbooks, 1977.

Cohat, Yves. *The Vikings: Lords of the Sea.* Ruth Daniel, trans. New York: Harry N. Abrams, Inc., Pub., 1992.

Crossley-Holland, Kevin. *The Poetry of Legend: Classics of the Medieval World: Beowulf.* Phoebe Phillips Editions, 1987.

Davidson, H. R. Ellis. *Gods and Myths of Northern Europe.* Baltimore: Penguin, 1964.

Delanty, Greg, Michael Matto, eds. Foreword by Seamus Heaney. *The Word Exchange: Anglo-Saxon Poems in Translation.* New York: W. W. Norton & Co., 2001.

Donaldson, E. Talbot. *Beowulf: A New Translation.* New York: Norton, 1966.

Fulk, R. D., Robert E. Bjork, and John D. Niles, eds. *Klaeber's Beowulf and the Fight at Finnsburg.* 4th Edition. Toronto: University of Toronto Press, 2008.

Garmondsway, G. N. *The Anglo-Saxon Chronicle.* London: J. J. Dent & Sons, 1972.

Godden, Malcolm and Michael Lapidge, eds. *The Cambridge*

Companion to Old English Literature. Cambridge: Cambridge University Press, 1991.

Heaney, Seamus, trans. *Beowulf: A New Verse Translation.* New York: W. W. Norton & Co., 2000.

Hollander, Lee M., trans. *The Poetic Edda.* 2nd ed. Austin, TX: University of Texas Press, 1990.

Klaeber, Fr. *Beowulf and the fight at Finnsburg.* Boston: D.C. Heath & Co. 1922.

Krapp, George Philip and Elliott Van Kirk Dobbie, eds. *The Anglo-Saxon Poetic Records: A Collective Edition.* 6 vols. New York: Columbia University Press, 1931-1953.

Niles, John D. *Beowulf and Lejre.* John D. Niles and Marijane Osborn, eds. Tempe, AZ: ACMRS, 2007.

Singer, Charles. *From Magic to Science.* New York: Dover Pub., Inc., 1958.

Sturluson, Snorri. *The Prose Edda: Tales from Norse Mythology.* Jean I. Young, trans. Berkeley: University of California Press, 1954.

Swanton, Michael, ed. and trans., *Anglo-Saxon Prose.* London: Everyman's Classic Library, 1993.

Tacitus. *The Agricola and the Germania.* H. Mattingly and S. A. Handford, trans. Harmondsworth: Penguin, 1987.

Weston, L. M. C. "Women's Medicine, Women's Magic: The Old English Metrical Childbirth Charms." *Modern Philology* 92 (1995): 279-293.

Further Reading

Allen, Michael J. B. and Daniel G. Calder, trans. *Sources and Analogues of Old English Poetry: The Major Latin Texts in Translation.* Cambridge: D. S. Brewer, 1976.

Barney, Stephen A. *Word-Hoard: An Introduction to Old English Vocabulary.* New Haven: Yale University Press, 1977.

Battaglia, Frank. "The Germanic Earth Goddess in Beowulf?" *The Mankind Quarterly* 31 (1997): 415-446.

Belanoff, Pat. "The Fall (?) of the Old English Female Poetic Image," *PMLA* 104 (1989): 822-831.

Bessinger, Jess B., ed. *A Concordance to Beowulf*. Ithaca: Cornell University Press, 1969.

Biggs, Frederick M. "The Politics of Succession in *Beowulf* and Anglo-Saxon Succession." *Speculum* 80.3 (2005): 709-41.

Birch, J. H. S. *Denmark in History*. London: John Murray, 1938; rpt. Westport, CT: Greenwood Press, 1975.

Bjork, Robert E. *The Old English Verse Saints' Lives: A Study in Direct Discourse and the Iconography of Style*. Toronto: University of Toronto Press, 1985.

Bright, James W. *Bright's Anglo-Saxon Reader*. New York: H. Holt and Company, 1917.

Bruce-Mitford, R. L. S. *The Sutton Hoo Ship-Burial: A Handbook*. London: The Trustees of the British Museum, 1968.

Calder, Daniel G. et al. *Sources and Analogues of Old English Poetry II: The Major Germanic and Celtic Texts in Translation*. Cambridge: D. S. Brewer, 1983.

Cameron, Angus. *Old English Word Studies: A Preliminary Author and Word Index*. Toronto: University of Toronto Press, 1983.

Cameron, M. L. *Anglo-Saxon Medicine*. Cambridge: Cambridge University Press, 1993.

Campbell, James, ed. *The Anglo-Saxons*. Ithaca, NY: Cornell UP, 1982.

Chance, Jane. *Woman as Hero in Old English Literature*. Syracuse: Syracuse University, 1986.

Damico, Helen. *Beowulf's Wealhtheow and the Valkyrie Tradition*. Madison: University of Wisconsin Press, 1984.

Damico, Helen and Alexandra Hennessey Olson, eds. *New Readings on Women in Old English Literature*. Bloomington: Indiana University Press, 1990.

Damico, Helen and John Leyerle. *Heroic Poetry in the Anglo-Saxon Period: Studies in Honor of Jess B. Bessinger, Jr.* Kalamazoo: Medieval Institute Publications, 1993.

Deegan, Marilyn and D. G. Scragg. *Medicine in Early Medieval England*. Manchester: Centre for Anglo-Saxon Studies, 1989.

Dockray-Miller, Mary. "*Beowulf*'s Tears of Fatherhood." *Exemplaria* 10.1: 29-50. 1-28.

Earl, James. "The Forbidden Beowulf: Haunted by Incest." *PMLA* 125.2 (2010): 289-305.

Fell, Christine with Cecily Clark and Elizabeth Williams. *Women in Anglo-Saxon England and the impact of 1066*. Oxford: Basil Blackwell, 1984.

Frantzen, Allen J. *Desire for Origins: New Language, Old English, and Teaching the Tradition*. New Brunswick: Rutgers University Press, 1990.

Frantzen, Allen J, ed. *Speaking Two Languages: Traditional Disciplines and Contemporary Theory in Medieval Studies*. Albany: SUNY Press, 1991.

Fulk, R. D. *Interpretations of Beowulf: A Critical Anthology*. Bloomington: Indiana University Press, 1991.

Glob, P. V. *Denmark: An Archaeological History from the Stone Age to the Vikings*. Trans. Joan Bulman. Ithaca, New York: Cornell University Press, 1971

Greenfield, Stanley B. *The Interpretation of Old English Poems*. London: Routledge and K. Paul, 1972.

Grohskopf, Bernice. *The Treasure of Sutton Hoo: Ship-Burial for an Anglo-Saxon King*. New York: Atheneum, 1970.

Hala, James. "The Parturition of Poetry and the Birthing of Culture: The *Ides Aglæcwif* and *Beowulf*." *Exemplaria* 10.1: 29-50.

Hall, John. *A Concise Anglo-Saxon Dictionary*. 3rd edition. Cambridge: Cambridge University Press, 1931.

Hamer, Richard, ed. and trans. *A Choice of Anglo-Saxon Verse*. London, 1970.

Harwood, Britton J. and Gillian Overing, eds. *Class and Gender in Early English Literature: Intersections*. Bloomington: Indiana University Press, 1994.

Hermann, John P. *Allegories of War: Language and Violence in Old English Poetry*. Ann Arbor: University of Michigan Press, 1989.

Huppé, Bernard. *The Web of Words*. Albany: SUNY Press, 1970.

Jember, Gregory K. *The Old English Riddles: A New Translation*. Denver: Society of New Language Study, 1976.

Joy, Eileen A., and Mary K. Ramsay, eds. *The Postmodern Beowulf: A Critical Casebook*. Morgantown: West Virginia University Press, 2006.

Kanner, Barbara, ed. *The Women of England: From Anglo-Saxon Times to the Present*. London: Mansell, 1980.

Klindt-Jensen, Ole. *Denmark Before the Vikings*. Trans. Eva and David Wilson. London: Jarrold and Sons Ltd, 1957.

Lapidge, Michael and Helmut Gneuss, eds. *Learning and Literature in Anglo-Saxon England*. Cambridge: CUP, 1985.

Lerer, Seth. "Grendel's Glove." *English Literary History* 61 (1994): 721-751.

Lerer, Seth. *Literacy and Power in Anglo-Saxon Literature*. Lincoln: University of Nebraska Press, 1991.

Lerer, Seth "'On fagne flor': The Postcolonial *Beowulf*." in *Postcolonial Approaches to the European Middle Ages: Translating Cultures*, edited by Ananya Jahanara Kabir and Deanne Williams, 77-102. Cambridge: Cambridge University Press, 2005.

Leyerle, John. "The Interlace Structure of *Beowulf*." In *Beowulf: A Verse Translation. A Norton Critical Edition*. Translated by Seamus Heaney and edited by Daniel Donoghue, 130-152. New York: W. W. Norton & Co., 2002.

Lord, Albert Bates. *The Singer of Tales*. Cambridge: Harvard UP, 1981.

Mitchell, Bruce, and Fred C. Robinson, eds. *Beowulf: An Edition*. Oxford: Blackwell, 1998.

Mitchell, Bruce and Fred C. Robinson. *A Guide to Old English*. New York: Oxford: B. Blackwell, 1986. 4th edition.

Oakley, Stewart. *A Short History of Denmark*. New York: Praeger

Publishers, 1972.

O'Brien O'Keefe, Katherine. "*Beowulf*, Lines 702b-836: Transformations and the Limits of the Human." *Texas Studies in Literature and Language* 23, No. 4 (1981): 484-494.

O'Brien O'Keefe, Katherine. *Visible Song: Transitional Literacy in Old English Verse*. Cambridge: Cambridge University Press, 1990.

Oswald, Dana M. "'Wigge under Wætere': Beowulf's Revision of the Fight with Grendel's Mother." *Exemplaria* XXI (2009): 63-82.

Overing, Gillian and Marijane Osborn. *Landscape of Desire: Parital Stories of the Medieval Scandinavian World*. Minneapolis: University of Minnesota Press, 1994.

Overing, Gillian. *Language, Sign, and Gender in Beowulf*. Carbondale: Southern Illinois University Press, 1990.

Parry, Milman. *The Making of Homeric Verse: The Collected Papers of Milman Parry*. Edited by Adam Parry. Oxford: Oxford University Press, 1987.

Sandner, David. "Tracking Grendel: The Uncanny in *Beowulf*." *Extrapolation* 40 (1999): 162-76.

Scragg, D. G. *Superstition and Popular Medicine in Anglo-Saxon England*. Manchester: Centre for Anglo-Saxon Studies, 1989.

Szarmach, Paul E., ed. *Holy Men and Holy Women: Old English Prose Saints' Lives and Their Contexts*. SUNY Series in Medieval Studies. Albany: SUNY Press, 1996.

Tolkien, J. R. R. "*Beowulf*: The Monsters and the Critics." In *Beowulf: A Verse Translation. A Norton Critical Edition*. Translated by Seamus Heaney and edited by Daniel Donoghue, 103-130. New York: W. W. Norton & Co., 2002.

Williamson, Craig. *A Feast of Creatures: Anglo-Saxon Riddle-Songs*. Philadelphia: The University of Pennsylvania Press, 1982.

Glossary

blood eagle: a form of torture and execution said to have been practiced by Vikings; the victim's ribs were broken and lungs pulled out, resembling bloody "wings"

byre: cow-house, shed

cot: cottage

degen: warrior or hero in Middle High German

dew-of-sorrows: blood

dew-of-wounds: blood

flyting: contest of words, often insulting

gift-stool: throne; used in *Beowulf* lines 168, 2327

glee: music, sport, play

gleeman: professional entertainer, itinerant minstrel

glory-twig: sword

hail-of-arrows: battle

half-years: way to order time; six months

helm-tree: warrior

lay: lyric or narrative poem meant to be sung

leech: doctor

leechbook: book with medical recipes

leechdom: a medical recipe

longboat: the style of boat used by the Vikings

mere: sea; lake, pond; mother

mew: the cry of a gull

night-rider: witch

peaceweaver: a term for the bride who unites two warring tribes; generally these marriages and the peace meant to follow such a marriage are doomed

poison-twig: sword

ringbreaker: king

rood: crucifixion cross; main speaker in the beautiful Old English poem, *The Dream of the Rood*

rune/runestave: one of the letters of the alphabet of the ancient Germanic peoples

scop: singer-poet; "sc" pronounced "sh"

season: half a year; way to order time

shield-tree: warrior

soul-slayer: Odin

thane: retainer to a king or lord; mutual loyalty is expected between lord and thane

torque: collar, armband, or necklace made of twisted pieces of metal

wergild: money paid in compensation for a crime

wolf-forest: battle

wolf-tree: gallows

worts: herbs, plants

wreckers: soldiers, fighters; from the Old English *wrecca* for adventurer or hero

wyrd: fate

Proper Names

Ælfsciene: Brimhild's aunt with magical and medical powers

Aeneas: Trojan hero

Æschere: counsellor to Hrothgar; killed by Grendel's mother in *Beowulf*

Æsir: the gods

Angel of Death: woman who helps in funeral rites as described by the Arab traveler Ibn Fadlan recounting what he saw on the banks of the Volga in 992

Atli: second husband to Gudrun, brother of Brynhild, also known as Attila the Hun

Aurvandil the Brave: husband of seeress; when one toe of his became frozen, Thor threw it up in the sky to become a star

Antiochus: incestuous father, king of Antioch in the Old English *Apollonius of Tyre*

Apollonius: hero of the Old English *Apollonius of Tyre*

Baldr: son of Odin, slain by Hoder, the blind god, Hoth, at Loki's instigation

Beadohild: daughter of King Nidhad (Old English) or Níthoth (Old Norse), from the Old English poem *Deor* and the Old Norse *Lay of Volund* where she is called Bothvild

Beowulf: hero of the Old English poem *Beowulf*; he is a Geat from southern Sweden.

Bikki: bad counselor to King Jormunrek[k] in the *Saga of the Volsungs*

Borgny: daughter of King Heithrek in *The Plaint of Oddrún*

Breca the Bronding: Beowulf's rival in a swimming contest as told about in *Beowulf*

Brynhild: Valkyrie and princess, beloved of Sigurd the Volsung, wife of Gunnar, sister to Atli, in the *Saga of the Volsungs*; also known as Brynhildr or Brunhild in the *Nibelungenlied*

Cassandra: daughter of the Trojan king Priam; said to have foretold the future but no one believed her

Coifi: original name of Jerome when still a pagan shaman; brother to Unferth; son of Ecglaf

Danes: Hrothgar's people

Dido: abandoned lover of Aeneas

Disir: female supernatural beings or guardian spirits

Eadgils: Swedish prince, son of Ohthere; later seeks revenge against Wiglaf, son of his brother's killer; referred to in *Beowulf*

Eadwacer: male figure in the Old English poem *Wulf and Eadwacer*

Ealhhild: Hrothgar's mother, Healfdene's widow

Eanmund: Swede, brother of Eadgils, killed by Weohstan, Wiflaf's father

Ecglaf: father of Unferth in *Beowulf* and Jerome

Ecgtheow: father of Beowulf, son-in-law of Hrethel; seeks Hrothgar's help after he kills Heatholaf before the start of the action in *Beowulf*

Edith: adopted daughter of Brimhild, mother of Sif

Elene: also known as St. Helen, mother of King Constantine, finds the crucifixion cross and the nails which impaled Christ in the Old English *Elene*

Erda: mother earth goddess and seeress

Erp: son of Gudrun and Jonak, killed by his brothers

Ethelwald: Brimhild's brother, Fara's son

Eve: consort to Adam in the Old English *Genesis B*

Fafnir: turned into a dragon and lies on the hoard of gold Sigurd eventually claims in the *Saga of the Volsungs*

Fara: a Jute, birth mother of Brimhild

Fenrir: son of Loki, a wolf who will break free and consume the sun at Ragnarök

Fjolsvith: giant watchman Svipdag encounters in the *Lay of Svipdag*

Franks: Germanic tribe who conquered Gaul

Freawaru: daughter of Hrothgar and Wealhtheow, peace-weaving bride to Ingeld in *Beowulf*

Freyr: god of fertility

Freya: goddess of love and fertility

Frija: wife of Woden; the Germanic Freya

Froda: father of Ingeld, Heathobard king

Froforgar: companion of Beowulf

Froði: king of Denmark, whose reign at the time of Christ's birth was said to have been extensive and peaceful

Geats: the tribe to which Beowulf belongs in southern Sweden

Gimlé: pagan heaven

Gjaflaug: tells Gudrun she is the most unhappy in *The First Lay of Guthrún* [Gudrun] (see **Gullrond** and **Herborg**). It's safe to say all the women suffered a great deal.

Glathsheim: the home of Odin

Gleipnir: the fetter used to restrain Fenrir

Grendel: the monster, said to be kin to Cain, in *Beowulf*; Beowulf kills him

Grendel's mother: the mother of the monster Grendel in *Beowulf*; Beowulf kills her

Grimhild: sorceress, mother of Gudrun and Gunnar, gives Sigurd the drink that causes him to forget Brynhild and later gives Gudrun a potion of forgetfulness in the *Saga of the Volsungs*

Gróa: wise woman, mother of Svipdag in *The Lay of Svipdag*

Gudrun: also known as Guðrún and Kriemhilt in the *Nibelungenlied*; daughter of King Gjuki, marries Sigurd; after his death is married unhappily to Atli; marries Jonakr; mother of Svanhild by Sigurd; she feeds to Atli her sons by him; sons by Jonakr named Hamdir, Sorli, and Erp

Gullrond: tells Gudrun she is the most unhappy (see **Gjaflaug** and **Herborg**)

Gunnar: brother to Gudrun, married to Brynhild, killed by Atli

Gunnhild: queen who curses Hrut at the start of *Njal's Saga*

Hæthcyn: son of Hrethel, brother-in-law to Ecgtheow, Beowulf's father

Hagbard: lover of Signy, put to death by her father

Halga: brother of Hrothgar, father to Hrothulf

Hamthir: son of Gudrun

Healfdene: father of Hrothgar; mentioned in *Beowulf*

Heathobards: Germanic tribe

Heatholaf: one of the Wylfings, killed by Ecgtheow before the start of *Beowulf*

Heith: a witch

Hel: daughter of Loki, rules the kingdom of death

Helga: slave, concubine of Unferth, mother to Skjold, sister to Inga

Helgi: son of Sigmund and Borghild, marries the Valkyrie Sigrún

Helm: ruled the Wulfings, according to the Old English poem *Widsith*

Helmings: Wealhtheow's family of birth

Heorot: means "hart," the hall built by Hrothgar in *Beowulf*

Herebeald: Geatish prince, uncle to Beowulf

Herborg: tells Gudrun she's the most unhappy in *The First Lay of Guthrún* (see **Gjaflaug** and **Gullrond**)

Hervor the Allwise: a Valkyrie

Hild: daughter of Hogni, lover of Hethin, her magic keeps the battle continuing

Hildeburh: wife of the Frisian king Finn in the tragic *Fight at Finnsburg* episode in *Beowulf*

Hildilid: adoptive mother to Brimhild

Holofernes: evil king of the Assyrians in the Old English *Judith*, a work appearing just after *Beowulf* in the Cotton Vitellius A XV manuscript

Hondscio: Geatish companion to Beowulf killed by Grendel in *Beowulf*

Hrethel: grandfather to Beowulf

Hrethric: brother to Hrothmund and Freawaru; son of Hrothgar and Wealhtheow in *Beowulf*

Hrothgar: king of the Scyldings or Danes

Hrothmund: one of the sons of Hrothgar and Wealhtheow

Hrothulf: nephew to Hrothgar, son of Halga

Hrut: victim of Gunnhild's curse at the start of *Njal's Saga*

Hygd: queen of the Geats and wife of Hygelac

Hygelac: king of the Geats and uncle to Beowulf

Hyndla: giantess

Idun: Inga's slave name

Inga: Helga's sister; beloved of Hrothulf

Ingeld: son of Froda, prince and later king of the Heathobards, husband to Freawaru in *Beowulf*

Jerome: adopted Christian name of Unferth's brother, son of Ecglaf; earlier known as Coifi the shaman

Jonakr: third husband of Gudrun, their sons are Hamdir, Sorli, and Erp

Jormunrek[k]: king of the Goths, jealous of his son Randver over Svanhild; has Randver hanged and Svanhild trampled to death by horses, from the *Saga of the Volsungs*; mentioned in the Old English poems *Widsith* and *Deor* as Eormanric

Judith: heroine of *Judith*, the Old English saint's legend following *Beowulf* in the Cotton Vitellius A XV manuscript; kills Holofernes by beheading him, thereby saving the Hebrew people

Judas: in the Old English *Elene*, helps St. Helena find the true cross and the nails which impaled Christ, converts and becomes the bishop Cyriacus; not the Judas in Scripture

Juliana: virgin martyr in the Old English *Juliana*

Loki: one of the Æsir, god of trickery

Midgard Serpent: the world serpent which breaks loose at Ragnarök; Loki is the father of the Midgard Serpent

Modthryth: has suitors killed until she marries Offa, either the fourth-century king of the continental Angles or the eighth-century king of the Mercians in England in *Beowulf*

Nástrandir: the strand of the dead or corpses, where Hel's home is located

Nerthus: Mother Earth goddess of the Germanic people as told by Tacitus in his *Germania*

Niflheim: beneath the roots of the World Tree, the realm of Hel

Njorth: he and his sister are the parents of Freyr and Freya; god of ships and the sea

Norns: the three fates, they rule the destiny of men

Oddrún: Atli's sister, helps Borgny give birth

Odin: god of battle, inspiration, and death; also spelled Óðinn or Óthinn.

Offa: either the fourth-century king of the continental Angles or the eighth-century king of the Mercians in England; marries Modthryth in *Beowulf*, also mentioned in the Old English poem *Widsith*

Onela: king of the Swedes, son of Ongentheow, presumably married to Yrse, daughter of Healfdene

Priam: king of the Trojans; mentioned by Snorri Sturluson in *The Prose Edda* as the grandfather of Thór

Ragnarök: the twilight of the gods; the end of the world when monsters slay the gods and the world of men and the home of the gods are destroyed

Randver: son of Jormunrek[k]; hanged by his father out of jealousy for Svanhild, daughter of Gudrun and Sigurd

Regin: urges Sigurd to kill his brother Fafnir

Rerir: grandson of Odin; received apple of fertility from Odin's wishmaiden; father of Volsung who lay in his mother's womb for six years and finally had to be cut from her; father of Sigmund

Sæwald: husband of Hildilid, adoptive father of Brimhild

Scyld Scefing: grandfather of Hrothgar in *Beowulf*; note: "sc" in Old English is pronounced like "sh"

Scyldings: another word for the Danes, Hrothgar's people in *Beowulf*

Scyldtheow: Hildilid's brother, one of the shore guard

Scylfings: another word for the Swedes who will eventually destroy the Geats after Beowulf's death in *Beowulf*

Sessrúmnir: Freya's hall

Sif: Brimhild's birth name; the name of her adopted grand-daughter and narrator of the novel; Thor's wife, has beautiful golden hair

Sigbert: father of Fara of the Jutes, grandfather of Brimhild

Siggeir: Signy's first husband; it is a very unhappy marriage; his mother transforms herself into a she-wolf to kill Sigmund, who succeeds in killing her with Signy's help; Sigmund kills Siggeir and his

Sigmund: son of Volsung, escapes from the she-wolf with Signy's help; mates with his sister Signy; father of Sigurd with his wife Hjordis; in the *Saga of the Volsungs*

Signy: daughter of Volsung; mates with brother Sigmund, their son is Sinfjotli; Signy elects to die with her treacherous husband Siggeir in a burning house

Sigrún: a Valkyrie, loves Helgi who dies killing her betrothed

Sigurd: son of Sigmund and Hjordis; kills the dragon Fafnir; awakes Brynhild and they swear their love; Grimhild gives him a potion of forgetting; he marries Gudrun; Brynhild unhappily marries Gunnar; the two women quarrel; Sigurd is killed; Brynhild lies on his funeral pyre; has daughter with Gudrun named Svanhild

Skathi: daughter of Thjasti the giant, wife of Njorth; prepares the venomous snake which drips its poison on Loki for his accusations of sleeping with him in *The Flyting of Loki*

Skjold: son of Unferth and Helga

Sorli: son of Gudrun and Jonakr

Sváva: Valkyrie, loves Helgi who, on his deathbed, bids her marry his brother, Hethin; she refuses

Svanhild: daughter of Sigurd and Gudrun; trampled to death by horses

Svipdag: son of Gróa; in *The Spell of Gróa* he receives spells from his mother to help him on his quest to enter a flame-surrounded castle

Thor: god of thunder, son of Odin; in the Prologue to Snorri Sturluson's *Prose Edda*, he is the grandson of the Trojan Priam and the ancestor of Odin

Unferth: counsellor to Hrothgar, son of Ecglaf, accused of being a brother-killer by Beowulf in *Beowulf*

Valhalla: hall of the slain

Valkyrie: choosers of the slain; they help the god of war Odin

Vingólf: sanctuary of the goddesses

Volsung: son of Rerir, father to Signy and Sigmund, killed treacherously by Siggeir

Wealhtheow: queen and wife to Hrothgar in *Beowulf*

Weders: another word for the Geats

Weland: blacksmith of the gods, also known as Volund

Widsith: scop of the Old English poem *Widsith* who speaks of having served dozens of kings and patrons; his name means wide-traveler

Wiglaf: loyal kinsman of Beowulf in *Beowulf*

Woden: God of battle and death worshipped by pagan Anglo-Saxons in England; the Old English form of Odin

Wolfgar: Hrothgar's herald and chamberlain

World Ash/World Tree: see Yggdrasill

Wulf: beloved in the Old English poem *Wulf and Eadwacer*

Wyrd: Fate

Wylfings: Beowulf's father, Ecgtheow, killed Heatholaf, a Wylfing, before the start of *Beowulf*; Hrothgar paid wergild to end the feud; Wealhtheow may be a princess of the Wylfings

Yggdrasill: forms the center of the gods, men, and giants, an ash tree; also known as the World Ash or World Tree

Ymir: the giant who is created from fire and ice; from his body comes the entire world

Also by Susan Signe Morrison

Women Pilgrims in Late Medieval England: Private Piety as Public Performance. London: Routledge, 2000. 978-0415221801

Excrement in the Late Middle Ages: Sacred Filth and Chaucer's Fecopoetics. The New Middle Ages Series. New York: Palgrave Macmillan, 2008. 978-1403984883

The Literature of Waste: Material Ecopoetics and Ethical Matter. New York: Palgrave Macmillan, 2015. 9781137405661

A Medieval Woman's Companion: Women's Lives in the European Middle Ages. Oxford: Oxbow Books, 2016.

Edited Book
Joan Wehlen Morrison. *Home Front Girl: A Diary of Love, Literature, and Growing Up in Wartime America*. Ed. Susan Signe Morrison. Chicago: Chicago Review Press, 2013. 978-1613744574

Visit the website for *Grendel's Mother* at
grendelsmotherthenovel.com

**TOP HAT
BOOKS**

Historical fiction that lives.

We publish fiction that captures the contrasts, the achievements, the optimism and the radicalism of ordinary and extraordinary times across the world.

We're open to all time periods and we strive to go beyond the narrow, foggy slums of Victorian London. Where are the tales of the people of fifteenth century Australasia? The stories of eighth century India? The voices from Africa, Arabia, cities and forests, deserts and towns? Our books thrill, excite, delight and inspire.

The genres will be broad but clear. Whether we're publishing romance, thrillers, crime, or something else entirely, the unifying themes are timescale and enthusiasm. These books will be a celebration of the chaotic power of the human spirit in difficult times. The reader, when they finish, will snap the book closed with a satisfied smile.